METEOR

A NEW WORLD ORDER

J.D. MARTENS

EPIC Escape

An Imprint of EPIC Press
abdopublishing.com

A New World Order
Meteor: Book #6

Written by J.D. Martens

Copyright © 2018 by Abdo Consulting Group, Inc.

Published by EPIC Press™
PO Box 398166
Minneapolis, MN 55439

Printed in the United States of America.

Cover design by Candice Keimig
Images for cover art obtained from iStock
Edited by Amy Waeschle

LIBRARY OF CONGRESS CATALOGING-IN-PUBLICATION DATA
Names: Martens, J.D., author.
Title: A new world order/ by J.D. Martens
Description: Minneapolis, MN : EPIC Press, 2018 | Series: The Meteor; #6
Summary: Jeremy and Anna encounter many difficulties in the new apocalyptic United
    States. Dustin and Karina also find themselves returning to their home country as Seed
    Ambassadors for the Global Seed Vault. Meanwhile, Robert and Major Winter are finding
    out that it will be much harder to leave North Korea than they had anticipated . . . Will
    civilization rise again after coming to the brink of destruction?
Identifiers: LCCN 2017946140 | ISBN 9781680768329 (lib. bdg.)
    | ISBN 9781680768602 (ebook)
Subjects: LCSH: Adventure stories—Fiction. | End of the world—Fiction.
    | Meteor showers—Fiction. | Teenagers—Fiction | Young adult fiction.
Classification: DDC [FIC]—dc23
LC record available at http://lccn.loc.gov/2017946140

For my parents, Bill and Laura,
who always encourage my passions

1

A NEW FUTURE

November 1, 2018, North Atlantic Ocean
Four and a Half Weeks to Impact

Dustin and Karina had been granted the right to leave the island of Svalbard. After about a month of working as lab techs for David and Esther Malka, the leaders of the Svalbard Global Seed Vault had asked for volunteers to become Seed Ambassadors to deliver copies of seeds to various parts of the world. Dustin and Karina jumped at the chance to leave the frigid Arctic island and were the first to apply to go to North America.

The reason for the Seed Ambassador project was that the Global Seed Vault wanted to expand its seed holdings in case something catastrophic happened to Svalbard. A second benefit would be to give the still-standing governments of the world a hand in feeding their now-starving populations. So they decided to send some of their personnel around the world to deliver seeds to those governments that still held power over their citizens.

Comet 2 and Comet 3 were still on their way, and those at the Global Seed Vault wanted to ensure that—on the small chance the comets hit Svalbard or the Arctic Ocean near it—there would still be diverse seeds around the world to help in the repopulation effort. The scientists at the Global Seed Vault estimated that around forty percent of the world's population perished from the first impact's primary and secondary effects.

The scientists at the Global Seed Vault had also created UV-A and UV-B resistant crops that they hoped would survive in Earth's new atmosphere, and the Seed Ambassadors brought these with them in addition to the un-genetically modified crops. It was their contribution to the problem of starvation that would soon grip most humans all around the world.

The ocean liner on which they were traveling would port on North America, where they would disembark, and then continue to Central and South America, round Cape Horn, and go up along the west coast of the two continents, until finally making its way across the Pacific to Japan. As Dustin looked out along the water of the Atlantic Ocean, he was struck by how similar the horizon looked before the comet. The indelible ocean, still unchanged in its vast mystery, made Dustin forget the devastation of the comet. The impact had changed landscapes all around the world, and the volcanic activity that it catalyzed had even created new islands, but the ocean itself continued fluctuating between raging tempest and tranquil existence.

Dustin could see that the ocean was a tiny bit browner than it had been when they crossed the Atlantic to go to Europe. *God, it was only two years ago,* he thought. Dustin smelled the salty air as he gripped the metal railing of the ship. The feeling of the metal flashed him back to when Lukas had stuck the cigarette into his neck, and he'd gripped the metal table as hard as he could to try to shut out the pain. He shuddered.

Dustin felt that maybe by leaving Svalbard, the specter of torture might kindly stay behind on that desolate island near the North Pole, but he was wrong. Lukas had ingrained himself in Dustin's mind from that brief hour several months ago, and as far as he knew, Astrid had committed a similar sin against Karina's consciousness.

Despite the constant thought of his torture by the hands of Lukas on Svalbard, Dustin felt positive about returning to his home country. They would be dropped off somewhere along the eastern sea-board, and then head south to the other states which still maintained some form of autonomy over their citizens.

Dustin and Karina were not the only people who volunteered to leave Svalbard on the container ship; there were perhaps ten other groups of Seed Ambassadors—people who would deliver original and genetically modified UV-B seeds around the world. Each group was given two large suitcases filled with seeds which would grow in the destination's climate, as well as the gene-altered seeds. Along with the seeds, they would be given a four-wheel drive BMW, extra gas, MREs (Meals-Ready-To-Eat), clothes, two pistols for protection, and road and physical maps of the United States. Dustin and Karina would be the first Seed Ambassadors to leave the ship.

On their seventh day on the ocean they saw land, but it was not the land they thought they'd see. The sea level had risen an astounding sixty feet! Karina joined him on the deck of the ship, and gasped. Almost all of Cape Cod was submerged.

"Provincetown's gone," Karina said, aghast, remembering the vacation her family took once.

Only the roofs of houses could be seen; the rest of the houses were underwater due to the rising sea levels. *The temperature sure melted the ice caps fast*, Dustin thought.

The ship sailed slowly through Massachusetts Bay toward Boston. Much of the islands were submerged. As the city came into view, Dustin's jaw dropped. The bottom five stories of downtown Boston's buildings were completely underwater! The ocean simply did not stop at the harbor—it snaked through the tall buildings like they weren't even there. The captain told Dustin and Karina that they would anchor in the bay, and then a smaller boat would take them to dry land.

They boarded the smaller vessel, a catamaran-style raft that would take them and their vehicle ashore. Dustin, Karina, and Joe, the driver of the ferry, started out from outside the South Boston neighborhood and sailed through the rows of houses and apartment complexes that poked out of the ocean.

"Jesus," Dustin muttered.

As they sailed through South Boston and made their way inland down Tremont Street, only the top stories of the three-story buildings lining the street were still above water. Destroyed buildings and a lone crane littered the horizon. The tsunami had destroyed much of downtown Boston, and though the John Hancock building had fallen, the Prudential Tower still stood tall amongst the dilapidated buildings near it. *I can't believe how sad it all looks*, Karina thought.

They continued sailing down the street into shallower water another two miles before they could disembark and drive their car down the ramp to the ground. They said a quick goodbye to Joe, who nodded and turned around, sailing back toward downtown Boston.

Dustin got in the driver's seat and they drove through some surface streets to make it to the Massachusetts Turnpike, which would put them on the way due west. As they drove, they weaved through uprooted trees fallen on the road, as well as pieces of metal from fallen buildings and overturned vehicles. They had to circumnavigate all this garbage and debris until finally they were forced to stop ten miles down the Turnpike. A large office building had collapsed over the road.

Dustin crossed over the median and drove the wrong way down the interstate. This gave Dustin a strange exhilaration. Even though laws were all but naught in this new post-comet world, Dustin still felt the same twinge of excitement when doing something illegal, like trespassing, or when he used to drive with passengers when he only had his learner's permit.

Having slept long hours on the ship, both Dustin and Karina were well rested for their journey, which would take a few days to complete if they drove fast and long enough. Their mission was to drive to Los Alamos, New Mexico, which now served as the de facto capital of the United States, where they could provide the U.S. government with seeds. In the event they found people along the way in need of seeds as well, they were to provide for them, but the bulk of their store should be placed in the care of the government.

So they chugged along, weaving in and out of the debris littering the road. Dustin watched broken cars, the felled trees, and the abandoned buildings fly by as he stared out of the windshield. Dustin remembered driving to Vail with Jeremy and Anna, and wondered if they were alive.

"So," Dustin asked, "do you think that Jeremy and Anna are alive?"

Karina looked up at Dustin from the map she was looking at and said, "I think we should go west on I-80 for a while, and then I-71. That'll take us to Columbus, Ohio. Then we can probably go to St. Louis via I-70, and I-44 and I-40 through Missouri and Oklahoma City to New Mexico. What do you think?"

Dustin narrowed his eyes, wanting a response to his original question. When Karina didn't reply and continued looking at the map, Dustin repeated himself.

"What about Jeremy and Anna? Why didn't you answer me?"

"Of course, we could go south and cross the Appalachians in Virginia, which might be better because there could be more food the more south we go. Then again, there might be more people, which could mean that we shouldn't . . . "

"Karina? What about our friends?"

Karina stopped looking at the map then and closed her eyes, a few tears falling out from them. She looked over at Dustin in a fit of despair and said, "Dead! Dustin, they're dead! What—you want me to say that I think they're still alive? Do you know how unlikely that is? They are dead. Jeremy and Anna are dead. What other option is there for them? I can barely believe *we* are alive, and you think there's a chance in Hell they are? God, how could they be?"

Dustin looked back at the road, thinking he should have kept his mouth shut.

"You're right," he said slowly, and then offered, "I'm sorry—maybe I shouldn't have brought it up. I think we should go though Oklahoma and Columbus."

"They are dead, Dustin . . . gone," Karina repeated bitterly.

Dustin couldn't think of anything to say, so he refocused on the road and drove. He tried to acclimate to the new feeling of being on land once again. The cold of Svalbard and the icy wind of the sea that had consumed his mind for months were now in the past, and Dustin felt a serene nostalgia for being back on his home soil once again. Though it was also cold outside Boston, it was nowhere near as cold as Svalbard. He surveyed the landscape of Western Massachusetts before him. He'd visited the area once before and remembered the lush landscape being filled with trees and green fields. Now he was greeted by dilapidated brown hills with bare blackened trees where once great pines and spruces and hemlocks stood tall. As Dustin drove down I-90 West, the area looked more like a science fiction portrayal of a Martian landscape, albeit a little more brown than red. As they got farther away from the ruins of Boston, the abandoned car frames and ghost towns became less frequent, and after a few hours, Karina took over as driver.

Eventually they settled on four-hour shifts, wanting to get to their destination as quickly as possible. Getting gas was simple enough, and they found themselves at an abandoned gas station somewhere in Ohio the first time they needed to fill up. The car's trunk was filled with gas canisters, allowing them an extra two gas tanks for them to drive on. Whatever dangers lurked in the shadows did not bother the duo the first night, but at sunset on their second night they were aware of some movements along the road. At first they wanted to give them seeds, but truth be told they were terrified, preferring simply to give the seeds to the authorities.

They were somewhere on the outskirts of St. Louis. Missouri looked brown and desolate—like the rest of the United States—with dead grass and gray skies, and the occasional broken-down car. Dustin couldn't see a bare tree for miles.

By the time they reached the city it'd become night, and they drove around the lightless mini-metropolis. As they crossed the Mississippi, Dustin could see the St. Louis Arch still standing tall. In some of the buildings close to the freeway, they could see fires glowing in the windows. Dustin got out a flashlight and pointed it toward one of the buildings, and he shuddered when he could see eyes staring back at him.

Maybe Jeremy and Anna really are alive, Dustin thought. He was about to voice this to Karina, but after remembering their previous conversation, decided against it. Hours later, the sunrise brought with it fantastic hues of purples and blues, the likes of which Dustin had never seen before. Weather had become more extreme and bizarre since the comet hit Earth, and though this brought freak storms to the area, it brought with it a sensational beauty as well. As the sunrise brought a seemingly infinite mix of shades behind them in the east, Dustin rubbed his eyes. They had been open too long and had begun to sting. It felt like gravity was working overtime on his eyelids, but he drove on.

By noon of their second full day of driving, the weather had changed dramatically. Ahead of them were swirling dark grey cloud formations, and by the end of the hour there was no blue sky left. The darkness of the sky brought an ominous feeling to the inside of the car, which seemed to be getting smaller as the clouds sunk lower. The clouds felt so low that Dustin felt a little claustrophobic. As they drove along, a small spiraling cloud formed slowly and descended down.

"Dustin, that looks like a tornado," Karina said warily.

"Wow, really?" Dustin's eyes widened. "It looks so small."

It did look small. The rotating cloud, lighter in color than the sky, was surrounded by quick, swirling wind that caused dust to fling up into the sky.

The small, light-colored dagger of a cloud quickly increased in size and began to darken as it sucked up the dust from the ground. Dustin and Karina watched from their car while, in only a matter of minutes, the swirling wind column turned into a devastating tornado, traveling quickly to the north, and looked to intersect Interstate 70—the road they were currently driving down.

"Should we stop?" Dustin asked, unsure. He had never seen or experienced a tornado before.

"Yes!" Karina said, and they slowed their car to a stop.

The tornado increased in size and the wind whipped the car. It was maybe a hundred yards from them now, and they could feel the car being pulled north by the force of the wind. The air screamed outside and Dustin felt nervous, and shifted the car into reverse to prepare for a getaway. As Dustin and Karina watched the tornado, they were both captured by its enrapturing beauty, which tore through the dusty field ahead of them. There were no buildings on this stretch of I-70, and the tornado gracefully glided northward.

Suddenly, a flash of lightning lit the dark day throughout the horizon, shortly followed by the massive boom of a thunderclap. Then it began to rain.

"Jesus," Dustin said, watching the weather turn. As he looked around, Dustin could spy more tornadoes touching down, kicking up wet mud and dirt in a ferocious rampage.

"Let's get out of here," Karina said fearfully, opening up the map.

Dustin put the car into gear and turned on the windshield wipers, which did little to help his visibility in the downpour. Dustin took a left to head south, away from the tornadoes. The road appeared to be an old farm road, and it was very muddy. Using the map, Karina assured Dustin that the road was not a dead end, and they drove down it amidst the howling wind. When they reached a T in the road, Karina barked a direction, making sure to incorporate both the map and the tornadoes in her decision. Dustin followed her orders and in a few minutes they both felt safer, located just out of the storm and on a highway once again.

"What the heck," Dustin said as they drove out of the rain. "It just stops right here. That is so weird."

It was true. As Dustin drove south on a small country road through what used to be farmland all around them, suddenly the intense rain stopped completely. When Dustin looked back he saw a wall of water crashing down on the ground—and yet his car, just inches from the rain, was now free. Dustin could see the line of the storm stretch down the farmland for miles.

2

SUNRISE

November 6, 2018, Houston, Texas
Twenty-seven Days to Lunar Impact

Jeremy woke up late on his cot and stretched his back. The one beside him, where Anna slept, was empty. Jeremy could hear Anna vomiting in the other room. Jeremy rubbed the sleep from his eyes and checked his watch: 10:15 a.m.

"Anna, are you alright?"

"Yeah, I'm okay," she called from the bathroom.

Jeremy walked over to the main room of the bunker under 1821 River Oaks Boulevard. There, he did his exercises. He did one hundred pushups and one hundred crunches, then he sat still and focused on his breathing, meditating for fifteen minutes. Then, he spent another ten minutes doing lunges and squats, and then he put on his "outdoor clothes." These consisted of a long sleeve shirt and sweatpants. He also put on thin gloves and a bandana, a hat, and sunglasses. The temperature varied constantly in their post-apocalyptic world, but in Houston it had been above a hundred degrees for a week. Despite this, it was more important to protect from the Sun's rays than to stay cool, so Jeremy had to cover every inch of his skin.

Jeremy checked the surveillance camera and saw no movement outside the bunker. Then he unlocked the hatch and stepped outside into the humid air. He'd found genetically modified UV-B resistant strains of tomatoes and potatoes in the hatch and had planted them in a patch of soil he had prepared in the mansion's backyard. To his surprise they had actually already started to bud. He could see little stalks poking out of the soil. The natural green color was a refreshing change from the post-comet world's browns and grays.

Jeremy walked to the edge of the property of 1821 River Oaks Boulevard and hopped over the fence. Then, he ran down the block and onto the golf course. The course was near the bunker, and before the comet had been one of the most expensive places to play golf in the state of Texas. Now it was just an open field of dirt. Still, Jeremy felt it was a calming place to go for a run, and he ran, occasionally stopping to do more pushups or a few lunges. He jogged up and down the little hills of the golf course until his clothes dripped with sweat.

As he returned to 1821 River Oaks, Jeremy stopped short to walk the rest of the way. He could hear his own breath and it felt warm as it ricocheted off his bandana and back to his mouth—a most unpleasant feeling. As he walked slowly back to the house, feeling the rays of the Sun through his clothes, a sound came to Jeremy's ears. It was a low buzzing sound, and during his time living at 1821 Jeremy hadn't heard anything like it in the ghost city of Houston. The low rumbling sound was unfamiliar to him, and Jeremy tried to perk up his ears to get a better idea of the sound's origin.

Jeremy hopped the fence back onto the front lawn of the 1821 house that now served as his foyer, and then walked over to the garage, which had a lower roof than the rest of the French-style home. With a deft jump he grabbed the gutter and pulled himself up to the roof, where the black slate absorbed the Sun's rays.

He squinted in the hot noonday heat down River Oaks Boulevard and spied a small column of black dust rising in the distance. It looked to be coming in the same direction as the sound, which he now realized was the purr of an engine.

Uh oh, Jeremy thought.

In the distance Jeremy spotted a small caravan of three cars, heading in his direction. Jeremy had not ventured too far away from the bunker because of Anna, and had not seen a soul in the month they had been there. He did not know if people occupied the other areas of Houston. Watching the caravan gave him an uneasy feeling, and he'd had enough experiences to know that whoever was driving those cars wasn't coming by for a chat.

He watched in apprehension as the cars turned onto his street. He had a sinking feeling that they were coming toward him and 1821 River Oaks Boulevard.

It's too much of a coincidence that they'd be coming here . . . unless they read Janice's message too, Jeremy thought.

Jeremy hopped down to the ground and raced to the bunker, taking the steps down two at a time. He found Anna doing a few limbering exercises of her own.

"Hey," she called. Her legs were almost in splits, and she was stretching to the side. "Good morning! Have a good run?"

"Anna, we need to go," Jeremy said, rushing to gather their personal items from the bedroom.

"What?" Anna said exasperatedly. "Jer, what's happening?"

Jeremy explained about the group of cars while packing their things. He silently wished he had time to wash the sweat from his body, but a shower just wasn't in the cards for him.

Anna rolled her eyes. "Jeremy listen, this is nuts. How would they even know we are here? Or get in to the bunker?"

"You know how Janice kept that message in Morse code blinking for months, despite me shooting the laser pointer at the Ark? Well, I think someone else has found it. Just now, from the garage roof, I saw three cars turning onto our road, and I don't know who else they are going to pay a visit to if it's not us. There's nothing else here."

Jeremy stopped packing and walked over to Anna, took her hands in his, and looked up into her eyes. "I'm not going to let anything happen to you. I think that car is coming for the bunker. I know it's not good for you to travel, but we have to go. We have to go now."

"Go where?"

Before Jeremy could answer, an alarm sounded inside the bunker. Jeremy looked toward the camera that showed the front door of the hatch and saw three burly-looking figures outside the hatch door. *It's a good thing I changed the password,* Jeremy thought. Anna gave a fearful yelp and together the two of them grabbed as many necessities as they could—clothes, gasoline, MREs, water, nuts, beans, seeds that Jeremy had not yet planted, two pistols, a large knife, a two-way radio, and two solar panels— and threw them into the Humvee.

Anna struggled to get into the passenger side of the car, holding her belly, which had just started to get a little rounder.

Jeremy took one last look at the camera, and saw the largest of the three figures place something near the camera, and then all three ran out of the camera's view.

A bomb, Jeremy thought, grimacing.

He jumped back into the Humvee, turning the ignition. He clicked the garage door button on the visor of the Humvee. It opened the back door of the hatch: a ramp that led to the garage. As Jeremy inched the Humvee up the ramp, there was a terrific bang behind them.

"They'll need another two minutes or so to get through," Jeremy yelled, his ears ringing from the explosion.

The Humvee was in the garage now, squeezed between the side and a sedan next to them. Unfortunately, the main house's garage door would not open when Jeremy pressed another button on the Humvee's visor. *We're going to have to drive through it,* he thought. *I've always wanted to do this!* He stepped on the gas, yelling, "Hold on!"

The garage door gave away easily as they crashed through it, covering their heads with their arms. Anna looked over at the three cars parked in front of 1821 River Oaks and noticed a few surprised faces inside, pointing at them, and then Jeremy turned onto San Felipe Street, and they were gone.

The couple got out onto the highway. Jeremy

looked behind him to make sure the cars weren't following them, then looked over at Anna. She had a small bag to vomit into in her hands as a precautionary measure. Jeremy scrunched up his face, wishing he could do something to help her.

"I'm sorry that with everything else, you're sick now with morning sickness."

"It's okay, baby. I'm getting used it to by now," Anna lied. You never got *used to* throwing up and feeling nauseous.

"So, where do you think we should go?" Anna asked with a little difficulty.

They were driving through the streets of Houston, and Jeremy turned onto a freeway. He didn't think the group would follow them, because they now had what they wanted—the bunker and all of its resources.

"I think we have three options," Jeremy began. "We can either go to Los Alamos, where Dr. Miller said the U.S. Government is. He said the people at

Los Alamos would take care of us. We also could go back to the Winter's mansion."

"And the third option?" Anna asked, as Jeremy had stopped talking.

"The third option is we do none of those things, and just go somewhere by ourselves."

Anna thought for a moment.

"What do you think?" she asked.

"I think Los Alamos. We don't know how everything is going with little Norman and it would be best if—"

"Norman?!" Anna gasped, appalled. "Norman! You can't be serious."

"Norman was my grandfather's name!" Jeremy protested.

"We can discuss this later, sweetie," Anna said patronizingly.

Jeremy rolled his eyes playfully. He was relieved to have escaped. "Yeah okay, but where do you think we should go?"

"I don't like the idea of trusting the government.

I'm afraid to sacrifice our freedom. They would probably take our rights away for the 'security' of the nation, or something."

"What about Norman though? He would be safer with them."

"Stop calling him Norman, Jer! We don't even know if he is a he! He could be a girl."

"Well, it would be best if you have a doctor. And Los Alamos is the de facto capital of the United States. They'll have the army there, and there are sure to be doctors, nurses, and all the medicine we could ever wish for. Dr. Miller might be there, too, and maybe we could find someway to help. The largest fracture of the comet should be hitting in around five weeks' time, I think."

Anna thought for a moment, and then agreed with Jeremy; Los Alamos was the best place to go. With that settled, they began driving north, toward Los Alamos, where the government of the once *United* States of America tried to fight off the comet as best they could.

The drive took nineteen hours because of the broken-down cars and the bad roads. They stopped three times to refuel. They did this by siphoning gas from abandoned cars along the edge of the freeway. They'd park alongside the abandoned car, and Jeremy would hop out and quickly insert a hose into the car's fuel tank. Then Jeremy would draw the gasoline out by sucking through the other end of the hose. Once tasting the foul fluid, he would push the end of the hose into the Humvee, and they would drain the car of fuel.

Despite the simplicity of the process, it was still a nerve-wracking ordeal. Some well-timed robbers could have easily spotted them, murdered them, and taken their Humvee without a second thought. But they were lucky.

The landscape changed little on their path, until the hills of New Mexico signaled they were now in the foothills of the Rocky Mountains. It was already the early morning hours before dawn. The air felt thinner from the increased altitude and drier than the Houston air.

Jeremy drove up the way Anna guided, through yet another ghost city—Los Alamos. It was a mysterious city—the birthplace of the atomic bomb. In middle school Jeremy remembered going with his parents to Santa Fe on vacation and they made a day trip up to Los Alamos. There was a small museum located in the middle of the city about the atomic bomb, and how it was necessary to end World War II. Jeremy remembered asking his father about the bomb, nicknamed Little Boy, that the U.S. dropped on Hiroshima.

"If we hadn't done that," his father had said, "it would have taken years, and hundreds of thousands of more lives, to invade Japan and get their surrender. Instead, the war in the Pacific was over in just one week."

"But the people in those cities," Jeremy remembered himself saying, "they were just people, right?

They weren't soldiers. We just killed civilians, tens of thousands of civilians . . . "

"No, no, they weren't soldiers," his father had said.

Jeremy listened to the monologue of his memory as they drove by the abandoned children's museum. Then they took a left and saw the Los Alamos National Laboratory, barely visible in the dim light of dawn. He drove up to the entrance of the complex, a large tollbooth-style gateway. All the tollbooths were closed, and Jeremy drove right through them, then right through a second set of tollbooths. The Sun had risen over the horizon completely now and illuminated the bleak-looking countryside.

After driving through the second set, Jeremy saw a large military Humvee driving toward them. Then, from a loudspeaker on top of the Humvee, a booming voice echoed out toward them.

"Stop your vehicle at once. This is the Army of the United States of America. Stop your vehicle. Put your hands on the wheel, in plain sight. Stop your vehicle. This is the Army of the . . . " The voice repeated.

Jeremy did as he was told and slowed to a stop in the middle of the road. The military Humvee, fitted with a huge machine gun, looked like it could have eaten their own vehicle for breakfast. A military officer, face and skin shielded from the sunlight, got out of the car with a gun pointed at them. He walked over, and Jeremy rolled down the window. For a quick moment it reminded him of before the comet, getting pulled over by the police. He had a sudden urge to ask the officer if he wanted to see his license and registration, but he held his tongue.

"Morning," Jeremy remarked casually.

"Who are you?" the military man asked coldly.

"Jeremy Genser. This is Anna Chenko. We were told this would be a safe place to go. We are friends of Dr. Robert Miller's and Dr. Suri Lahdka."

It was difficult to tell what the man thought about this since his face was obscured by cloth, but he did not lower his weapon. The man turned slightly toward Anna.

"Dr. Miller is not here anymore."

"Yeah—he told us he went to North Korea. But he told us that if we ever got into trouble, we could go here."

"Stay here, and keep your hands on the wheel so I can see them."

The soldier pulled out a camera and took a photo of them. Then the soldier aimed the gun at Jeremy again. Jeremy was sure to keep his hands on the wheel but reminded himself that the pistol was just under his seat should he need it.

A second soldier marched up to Jeremy's car, took the camera from the first soldier, and walked back to their Humvee. Jeremy could see the soldiers using a short wave radio.

Then Anna let out a breath of relief as the soldier next to their Humvee slowly lowered his weapon.

"Follow our Humvee," he said.

After five minutes of following the truck, Jeremy

could see two figures in the distance, both with their arms crossed. It was difficult to make them out looking through the dust of the Humvee. They were heading toward these two shapes—a sort of welcome party for them. As they pulled up, Jeremy felt a little uneasy, since the people/soldiers were covered in clothing from head to toe, so he couldn't identify them. Would he and Anna be taken prisoner, or would they be allowed to join the Los Alamos community? Jeremy felt quite nervous for little Norman, swimming peacefully in his warm home in Anna's belly.

3

REUNION

November 7, 2018, Los Alamos, New Mexico
Twenty-six Days to Lunar Impact

Suri stood watching the vehicles kick up dust on its way back to the National Laboratory. Secretary Brighton stood next to her, his arms crossed. They watched as the Humvees swam through the dust, kicking up trails high in the air.

Ten minutes earlier, Suri had been with Secretary Brighton discussing an anomaly in Dr. Rhodes's data about Comet 2 when a haggard-looking soldier interrupted them, saying that there was a Humvee driving toward the National Laboratory. In it were two civilians in their early twenties.

"Capture them," Brighton had said, and Suri immediately protested.

"They haven't done anything wrong," she objected. "Can't we just see who they are, and what they want first?"

"That's why we are capturing them and not shooting them," the secretary returned nonchalantly, but nodded back to the soldier, who stood at attention, awaiting his orders.

"Find out who is in the car," Brighton said. "Now, what is this about Comet 2? Is this something we need to worry about?"

"Dr. Rhodes still has four nuclear weapons which she can deploy on the Vishnu spacecraft, so she is going to deploy two of them. This should ensure a more direct hit with the Moon."

"So be it," Secretary Brighton answered. *Scientists,* Secretary Brighton thought, annoyed, *they never speak in absolutes.*

"They know Dr. Miller, sir," the soldier's voice from the two-way radio rang out.

As if to himself, Brighton lamented, "Dr. Miller is not here anymore."

The soldier repeated what the Secretary had said, while Suri looked over at Secretary Brighton staring off into space.

They really got to be close friends, Suri thought, and suddenly she started to think about Robert, and how, if all went well, he'd be back on a plane home in just over a month.

"They say they are friends of Dr. Miller and Suri Lahdka," the soldier said to Secretary Brighton, "Jeremy Genser and Anna Chenko—"

"Jeremy!" Suri cried in surprise, and then repeated incredulously, "Jeremy Genser?"

Secretary Brighton looked back at Suri and asked, "You know him?"

Five minutes later, Suri stood alongside Secretary Brighton in the punishing sunlight, waiting for the duo to arrive. Within a few minutes Suri could see a bearded Jeremy and a tired and pale-faced Anna get out of the car.

"I can't believe you guys are here!" Suri exclaimed excitedly.

Suri ran up to hug them both.

"I can't believe it either," Jeremy admitted.

"Well, you're safe now," Suri said. "Come on, I'll find you a place to stay."

Suri was happy to see Jeremy's familiar face, and she led him inside the National Laboratory. Being so far away from the only useable launch station on the planet made her feel increasingly useless, as Robert needed her less and less as the days came closer to the comet's approach. Because Dr. Rhodes and Robert were monitoring Comet 2's trajectory, she was beginning to turn her attention to Comet 3. It was orbiting with Comet 2, but was so far away from it that it would not hit the Moon, instead going by it and hitting Earth shortly after Comet 2's lunar collision. Luckily, its damage would be minimal compared to the first impact.

The west wing of the complex of the National Laboratory had been converted into a living area, and this is where she took the two travelers. Suri thought that both of them looked remarkably healthy for having lived by themselves for four months. Suri noticed that Anna had a conspicuous tummy bump. *Oh wow*, Suri thought. Anna was pregnant? *They are so young!* It made her strangely happy to know that life would begin amidst all this horror. They needed something beautiful after everything. She resolved to do everything she could to make sure they were taken care of.

Suri took them to a corner of the cafeteria and made them each a cup of coffee. It was powdered instant coffee, but Jeremy and Anna hadn't tasted the black liquid in months, so the taste had a refreshingly nostalgic tang to it.

"So is this where the government is now?" Anna asked.

"Basically, yes," Suri answered, "There are a few thousand people living here, mostly NASA scientists and high-ranking government officials, along with some military officers, doctors, engineers, and some other essential personnel. There are other pockets of Americans living around the United States, but the de facto capital is this facility here. Underneath the facility—and under the nearby San Antonio Mountain—the government built enormous housing complexes."

"What about food?" Jeremy asked.

Suri stirred her coffee.

"Some of the botanists are trying to plant some vegetables and grains in the soil. We also have a massive store of grains and MREs—but eventually we'll have to start growing our own food again."

Jeremy noticed that the scar on Suri's face from her accident looked almost completely faded away compared to the last time he'd seen it.

When Jeremy told her this, she responded, "Oh wow, that seems so long ago."

"So much has happened since then," Jeremy said, struggling to articulate what was going through his head. *Everything has happened since then*, he thought.

"Yeah," Suri said.

"What's going on with the two other fractured comets?" Jeremy finally asked after an awkward silence.

"We are pushing the second comet to come into a direct impact with the Moon, so that will take care of that one. The Moon will absorb the impact, so we'll avoid it completely."

"Wow, that seems risky, right? Wouldn't it maybe change the orbit of the Moon?" Jeremy asked.

"Oh no, Comet 2 is much too small to change the Moon's orbital path. The Moon is so large in comparison to the comet that it won't change it at all. Not even the Earth's tides will be affected."

"Wow, that's amazing."

"What about the other comet, the last piece?" Anna asked. She noticed there was a small jar with a little spoon in it on the table adjacent to them. "Is that sugar?" she asked, excitedly.

"Yes! Oh, you probably haven't had sugar in a while, right?"

Anna rushed over to the table and grabbed the jar,

putting three spoonfuls of the sweet crystals into her coffee. Jeremy excitedly did the same. *Sugar,* Anna thought, *how I missed you.* The sweet taste was a flavor explosion.

"I've been craving this so much, especially since I'm—" Anna paused, not sure if she should confide in Suri.

"Pregnant?" Suri finished.

"How'd you know?" Anna asked.

Suri shrugged. "You're sort of showing," she said.

Anna looked at her belly and grinned. "I guess I am."

"Congratulations," Suri said. "That's so great—for both of you," she said.

"Thanks!" Anna responded.

Jeremy smiled warmly at Anna, but inside, all he felt was apprehension. *Apocalypse child—talk about a bad world to bring a child into,* he thought. A long silence followed. Jeremy squeezed Anna's hand.

"So, uh, about the comet," Suri continued. "It's only about a kilometer in diameter. It should do much less damage than the first impact. It won't affect global climate; most likely it will be a regional threat. It should land somewhere in the South Atlantic Ocean."

Jeremy nodded.

"Shall we walk?" she asked, rising. "I can give you a tour around the complex and then show you to your rooms. After that I'll have to get back to work."

They took their coffees and walked through the cafeteria and down a narrow hallway lined with what used to be labs, lecture halls, conference rooms, and oversized closets. These had been converted into bedrooms for some of the scientists and engineers living at the National Laboratory.

Suri took them to a door at the end of the hallway and opened it to what probably used to be an unforgettable view of the great wooded foothills of the Colorado Rockies. The woods were now those familiar spike-shaped remnants of trees. The red sandstone still protruded from the hills, and the mountains lay behind them.

"The soil is still good for planting, according to the plant biologists here, but every few weeks we have a bout of acid rain that they say discontinues any plant growth. Coupled with the intense UV sunlight, even if the buds were to break the surface of the Earth, it's likely they would be incinerated by the increased amount of ultraviolet radiation coming from the Sun," Suri said, looking out over the hills through her pair of aviators. She had purchased them from the gift shop at the Los Alamos Historical Society.

"I was able to grow a little bit in Houston; thankfully we didn't have any acid rain. It's a new world we live in," Jeremy mused, before asking, "Is this really the whole U.S. government, and was that really Secretary Brighton? The Secretary of State?"

"Yeah, it is—and yes that was him. President Chaplin is also here. After the anarchists gained power, the Chaplin Administration decided that the comet was a more important enemy to the United States than anything else, and they focused all their energy on getting Dr. Miller and me what we needed to defeat it. It's sad, but there are perhaps only a few thousand here in Los Alamos. There are a few other localized authorities, but I'm not sure to what extent the government here is communicating with them. I'm guessing the fragments of the U.S. government will rejoin once the comet situation has been taken care of. Everyone is still so scared that the larger fragment will hit us. And North Korea has the only workable launch facility in the world, so a lot of the engineers can only advise North Korea on what to do next."

Suri looked and spoke diplomatically, and she sounded much more confident than when Jeremy had first met her back in Houston.

"Do you think we'll be able to rebuild?" Jeremy asked.

"Rebuild what?" Suri asked.

"Everything," Jeremy answered.

Suri did not say anything for a long moment while she looked out over the horizon. At last she spoke, "Eventually, but only partially . . . we are back to pre-industrial times even now. It's like we had a hero from the future bring us all these fancy gadgets, but no way to turn them on. Plus, the entire country aside from our little complex is undoubtedly experiencing deadly food shortages. We are doing what we can to start farming again. We are lucky now to have clean water for the moment—since much of our water sources are underground. But the acid rain around the country has likely contaminated the above-ground rivers that people may be using for drinking water, which isn't good."

Suri sighed.

"I don't know," she continued, "it's going to take a long time for the entire world to recover from this. If it ever does."

• • •

Janice sat in her customary location eating lunch with Alex, whom she had grown quite fond of. Alex was truly her only friend on the Ark, though she still felt guilty about using him. She'd hacked into his Ark login account and changed the angles of the solar panels to reflect a message in Morse code to Earth. In the end, as Janice had suspected, Alex had discovered the changed code and couldn't understand how it had happened. He had been bothering Janice about it for weeks.

"It just doesn't make any sense," Alex was saying for the tenth time. "Who would insert a random code into the solar panel algorithm?"

Janice shrugged.

"Maybe it's just someone trying to sabotage the Ark or something?" Janice said nonchalantly. "Or maybe it's someone who figured out how to access the Ark's servers from Earth!"

"Yeah, maybe," Alex responded, unconvinced.

Janice took a bite of her vitamin mush—her third helping in as many days.

"I am sure I didn't do this. How could it have

changed? What is the purpose of this?" Alex mumbled.

Janice was doing her best to keep him away from the truth. It wasn't just because she wanted him to like her—which she did—but she also wanted to protect him. This way he would not be at fault if she were found out. Ignorance is bliss.

This did not, however, keep Alex from searching for the source of this mysterious scrap of code.

They finished their dinner together and decided to go toward the observation deck, which often was quiet right after dinner. This was because the observation deck was not part of the artificial gravity area of the Ark. It took a little getting used to the zero gravity feeling, particularly when having a stomach full of food, and was probably what kept most people away. However, they could also count on being alone there, and combined with the stunning view of the stars and Earth, this made the observation deck one of the most romantic places on the Ark. They embraced tightly and kissed each other, and Janice asked Alex, "Do you want to go back to Earth with me?"

"What do you mean?" Alex asked, confused.

"I'm tired of living up here. We know where the bunker checkpoints are. We can use one of the escape pods."

"What about the two comets?"

"They aren't big enough to entirely destroy Earth . . . " Janice trailed off, suddenly losing some of her momentum in trying to convince Alex of her want to leave.

Alex looked over Janice's face for some sign that would elucidate her feelings on the matter, but came up empty.

"Why leave?" he asked.

"Why stay, Alex? Do you like it up here? Do you like only being able to move around on this ship? Do you like any of this?"

"No," Alex admitted, "but it probably wouldn't be smart to leave now. Why not wait for the comets to hit Earth before we leave?"

"Well," she began, "if we go now we can choose to go whenever we want, and those here might not expect us to do it. We would be free to live away from these people and free to start a life. If we wait, I'm sure that Mr. Kaser will have a plan, which we will have no choice but to follow, and who knows what that might be. Plus, you heard Mr. Kaser last week—they said that NASA is trying to shoot the Moon with the comet. If we assume they succeed, then there's no reason why we shouldn't just go down to Earth now."

"If they succeed," Alex repeated, unsure.

But Janice could see Alex considering the option, and certainly it helped that they were locked in a tight embrace. After she had thought to leave the Ark a few weeks ago, Janice had been confused as to why the thought hadn't occurred to her earlier. It made perfect sense, since the remaining two comets were not capable (insofar as she knew) of destroying the Earth, she hated living on the Ark itself, and she had the locations of the checkpoints in the event she really did need some extra help.

"I have heard some others talking about abandoning the ship to go back, and take whatever punishment the comet doles to the Earth," Alex said abruptly, while Janice was still in thought.

"Oh really?"

"Yeah. People are eager to get off this ship."

"I can't imagine why."

"Seriously," Alex agreed, "though this view is breathtaking."

They floated in silence for a while enjoying each other's company and gazing at the Earth and at all the stars surrounding it. Being in the viewing deck gave life on the Ark an entirely different aura—one of mystery, the vastness of the universe, and the perpetuity of time. No matter what happened to that little blue-green orb, the universe would keep on ticking.

4

SURPRISE

November 10, 2018, Los Alamos, New Mexico
Twenty-three days to Lunar Impact

Jeremy's experience with electrical work was coming in handy. He spent the days at the Los Alamos National Laboratory fixing electrical equipment. Before it was the Johnson Space Center, then Major Winter's mansion, and now it was the Los Alamos National Laboratory, but the work was the same.

As for Anna, now that she was in her third trimester she had her energy back and wasn't nauseous. But her belly was increasing in size; almost every day it seemed to get larger. *This little human wants to grow up fast*, Anna thought.

Amongst the scientists and other people living at the Los Alamos facility, Anna had become a kind of a celebrity. She had arrived out of the blue, pregnant and healthy from the wasteland of anarchy surrounding the United States' safe zone. The frequent stares she received had started making her feel uncomfortable, so she spent her time in the library, reading up on anything she could get her hands on. She found one book called *Unconventional Birthing Methods*, so mostly she buried her head there.

When not in the library and when Jeremy had free time, the two of them would seek out Suri. Together they would discuss the fate of the United States—and the world—about what was to come of their planet. They spent sleepless nights discussing the new anarchy and what had to be a drastic focus on agriculture.

"People need to eat, and we can't live off the MRE meals forever. We will need to plant crops and start to rebuild," Anna said as they sat in the lobby of the National Laboratory. The lobby now served as a sort of meeting point for many people after working hours. It was the most beautiful of the rooms in the complex, and it was filled with comfortable couches, where they now sat. Suddenly a soldier jogged by them, speaking into his microphone.

"Who are they? They're from where?" The soldier said into his two-way radio.

Jeremy listened for more, but nothing came, and he turned to Suri.

"What do you think you'll do, Suri? I mean, once all of this is over?" Jeremy asked.

Suri looked downcast and thought for a long time how to respond to the question.

"Well, my study and life's work have made me pretty important to the whole stopping the comet affair, but if things turn out to be okay and the Moon successfully shields us from Comet 2, I'm afraid I won't be of much use anymore. I'm not sure what I'll do then."

"They'll probably build a huge statue of you,"

Anna offered. "I mean, you did basically save the entire world, and maybe all life, even. You've definitely saved my little—"

"Norman!" Jeremy interrupted eagerly.

Anna rolled her eyes.

"Jeremy!" she said, exasperated, "I told you, we are not naming our baby Norman! We don't even know the sex yet."

Suri laughed at the couple, smiling.

"Well, I don't know if I've saved your baby, but thank you. That baby is going to have an interesting life in this new world."

"Ain't that the truth," Jeremy agreed.

After a little idle conversation, Suri excused herself to go to sleep, and Jeremy and Anna followed suit. They walked together to their room, which was small, but at least it consisted of a bed large enough for them both to sleep on. It was a welcome upgrade compared to the cots they'd slept on in the bunker in Houston.

Jeremy slept like a baby, and while he

unconsciously took up most of the bed, Anna woke up frustrated with one of his hands in her face. It was her third night in a row waking up to go to the bathroom. Her natural sleep position was on her stomach, but it was too uncomfortable to do that now that her belly was growing.

The next day, Anna had an appointment with one of the government doctors to discuss her pregnancy. The woman's name was Dr. Patricks, and they met in a laboratory to discuss her symptoms and to ensure everything was on track.

Dr. Patricks was a middle-aged woman from Oregon with a kind face and too many wrinkles, making her look a great deal older than she probably was.

After the examination, Dr. Patricks put her stethoscope around her neck again and said, "Well, for now, everything looks great. Your weight is fine, everything seems stable. I'll just take your blood pressure, now, okay?"

"Sure," Anna replied.

She strapped the inflatable cuff to Anna's arm.

"So, what did you do before you came here to Los Alamos?" Anna asked.

"Well, I'm a licensed MD," Dr. Patricks answered, "but I started out as a botanist." Dr. Patricks gave Anna a warming smile.

"Really?" Anna said, excited that she and her doctor might have something in common. She waited while the doctor stuck half the stethoscope into her ear.

"Yes. And, actually," Dr. Patricks said after listening for her pulse and releasing the cuff, "because of that background, I've just been asked to help with a new project. Yesterday, another couple came to Los Alamos and brought us a trunk full of natural and genetically modified seeds. Apparently, they are Seed Ambassadors." She wrapped the cuff up and tucked it back into a drawer.

"Wow," Anna said.

"I'm going to help by confirming the genetic modifications and predicting their reproductive speed. We don't want to accidentally populate the United States with some weird form of mutant corn or something—then all the other plants wouldn't survive."

"Where did the couple come from?" Anna asked.

"You know," Dr. Patricks said, "it's interesting you ask that, because they're American, but they came from the Svalbard Global Seed Vault, which is north of Europe. They're young, like you and Jeremy, a man and a woman."

"Huh," Anna replied. "They came yesterday?" Anna remembered the soldiers streaking past them the night before.

"Yeah, they did. They're in the holding room right now, actually, on floor B3."

"Do you remember their names?" Anna asked.

"No, sorry. A girl, Hispanic I think, from Houston. The guy had a nasty scar on his forehead, and black hair."

It couldn't be . . .

"I need to go," Anna said, and jumped down from the exam table.

"Wait, we still have to talk about—"

"I'll be right back, Doc, I'm sorry. I know it's a long shot but I just have a gut feeling."

Anna started running to the stairs, feeling alive with purpose.

Could it be them? Anna hoped. *Please be them.*

When she got down to floor 3B, she found a guard holding a gun. He moved to stand in the way.

"I'm sorry, miss, but you can't go in here. Restricted Area."

"Are you keeping the young couple who came here yesterday?" she asked, out of breath. "The two who came from the Global Seed Vault?"

"I'm sorry, miss," the guard returned, "but this is a restricted area. I'm going to have to ask you to leave."

Anna tried to look down the hallway, which was filled with cell-like doors on both sides. Suddenly, the elevator door opened, and the Secretary of State walked out of it, holding a briefcase.

"Secretary Brighton!" she called. "Secretary!"

The old politician looked weary when he looked over in Anna's direction.

"You're Dr. Miller's friend, Anna, correct?"

"Yes," Anna replied.

"What are you doing down here? This is a restricted area."

"I know. But those two people that came to the facility yesterday, can I see them?"

"No, I'm sorry, Anna. Now, if you'll excuse me—"

"No—wait, please! Are you seeing them now?"

But the secretary had already turned to leave, walking down the hallway.

Screw it, Anna thought.

"Are their names Dustin and Karina? They both have black hair? Are they both from Houston and they traveled to Europe before the impact hit?"

Secretary Brighton stopped in his tracks, and turned around.

"Who told you that?" Brighton asked roughly.

"I—no one," Anna answered. "I went to high school with them. Jeremy and I lived with them in my cabin in the Rockies when the government first made the comet public knowledge. They're my friends. They're U.S. citizens. Please don't hurt them, let them come in."

Secretary Brighton looked down at the young woman pleading with him to see her friends, and he sighed.

"Your friends are okay, and they're safe. We just need to get some more information from them. Now—I need you to go back upstairs. You can see them in the afternoon."

Secretary Brighton nodded to the soldier, who backed Anna up toward the stairs.

Anna walked up toward the cafeteria to try to find Jeremy. By the time she reached him seated at a table in a far corner of the cafeteria, she was sobbing.

"Oh my God, Anna, what's wrong?" Jeremy asked. "Is there something wrong with the baby?"

Anna smiled through her puffy eyes. "No, no, everything's alright. It's . . . it's Dustin and Karina. They're here. They arrived here yesterday."

"What?!" Jeremy asked, bewildered.

He asked Anna a million questions but Anna couldn't answer any of them.

Then, he started to cry, too.

"Did you see them?" he asked.

"No, but we can go down in the afternoon."

I can't believe it, Jeremy thought. Jeremy and Anna waited as long as they could, and then they hustled back down to the floor where Dustin and Karina were being held.

"They're going to be so surprised!" Jeremy said excitedly.

The last time he had seen them they were boarding a ship to the European mainland, and that was before the first comet had hit.

Jeremy and Anna took the elevator down to floor

3B and they waited anxiously behind the guard until the door to one of the holding cells opened and Secretary Brighton walked out holding his briefcase.

"Let them through," he called.

Slowly they walked toward the holding cell, and opened the steel door. Dustin and Karina were sitting on the same side of a small interrogation table, looking tired.

"I can't believe you guys are really alive!" Jeremy said excitedly.

Dustin and Karina's jaws dropped. Jeremy ran over to Dustin and hugged him tightly.

"Oh my God, what happened to your faces?" Anna asked as she did the same, but the question was drowned out by Karina, who began to cry uncontrollably.

"Jesus," Anna sobbed. "I just stopped crying."

It had been two years since they had seen each other, but Dustin seemed at least a decade older. Karina's dark hair had grown long enough to hang down her back.

Dustin looked similarly amazed, surprised, positively stupefied that Jeremy was looking at him in the middle of New Mexico.

"I knew it!" Dustin said triumphantly. "I knew he was still alive. You said they were dead but I knew he was alive," Dustin repeated, smiling over to Karina.

Karina also looked befuddled and giddy at seeing Jeremy, and they traded hugging partners.

From the door, Secretary Brighton smiled inwardly at the good fortune that he saw, for it was not every day that something good happened in the new world.

The two couples smiled warmly at each other for another minute, hugging each other, and then they each went over what had happened to each other over the past two years. Dustin and Karina went first.

Dustin composed himself, and Jeremy, still wearing a smile on his face, listened intently to Dustin and Karina as they explained how they had landed somewhere in The Netherlands and eventually traveled to the Svalbard Global Seed Vault (the SGSV). Then, they were tasked with sending over a trove of natural and genetically modified seeds to the government, who the SGSV had lost communication with some months before. Secretary Brighton also listened intently from the door. When he had heard enough, he spoke up. It made the four old friends jump, since they had forgotten Secretary Brighton was still there.

"Jeremy, these two have had a long night of questioning by our intelligence department. Maybe you could take them to their room? They'll be two doors down from you. I have some other work to take care of."

"Thank you so much, Mr. Secretary," Dustin replied.

Secretary Brighton nodded then departed. Dustin then filled him in on some of the things about the trip that he did not tell to Secretary Brighton, such as the uneventful drive from Boston to Los Alamos.

"I think more people survived than we thought,"

Dustin replied. "In the United States—and the world—so we'll have help in the rebuilding process."

As they walked back to their floor, Jeremy explained their story of the past two years. Anna ended the tale by telling Karina she was pregnant!

"Oh my God, Anna! Congratulations!" Karina screamed, and hugged Anna.

"Thanks!" Anna replied warmly.

"I can't believe you're actually pregnant, Anna. I knew you were alive!" Dustin remarked.

"Thanks, yeah it's been a hectic couple of months. Hey, what happened to your face, Dustin?" Anna asked.

"Yeah, what did happen to your face?" Jeremy asked.

But for the second time, Dustin ignored the question. Anna continued to ask them about their time abroad and they traded stories about all of their adventures over the past year, just happy to be together again.

• • •

Robert and Major Winter had been transferred a week earlier from their cushy hotels to a detention center inside the Pyongsong launch facility. Robert knew this was bad—the North Koreans were holding him as leverage for nuclear and ballistic secrets from the United States. It was stupid to think that Major Winter could protect him since he was being held hostage, too.

"I think it's time for me to go back home," Robert said calmly to Mr. Yuan, his Korean translator. "There's just under three weeks before Comet 2 hits the Moon, and we don't have the capacity to build any more missiles and launch them before the Lunar Impact. I've served my purpose here."

"Dr. Miller," Mr. Yuan said, sighing, "I do not think you fully appreciate the situation. The Supreme Leader would like your help furthering the nuclear technology of the great state of North Korea.

We would like to make a Hydrogen bomb, and fit it to an intercontinental ballistic missile. We require your assistance."

"I already told you," Robert said rubbing his temples, "I'm not a nuclear engineer. I don't know how to make an atomic bomb. I'm an astrophysicist. Yes, I worked with the construction of the IMPs which—yes—did have nuclear weapons on them. I only configured them to work with rockets that were specially designed to send them into space. Not all physicists can split the atom. And anyway, why do you need more weapons? So many have died already, Mr. Yuan."

Mr. Yuan sighed deeply at this, and Robert thought it was sweet that the young man cared so much for him that he would be sad to see him leave. It was with dismay that he realized Mr. Yuan was sad for an entirely different reason.

"I'm sorry, Dr. Miller, I truly am," Mr. Yuan said, before giving Dr. Miller an envelope.

Dr. Miller frowned and flipped open the

envelope, and looked inside. What he found surprised, angered, and frightened him immensely.

"Jennifer . . . " he whispered.

I don't believe it, Robert thought, but he looked more closely at the contents of the envelope. There were three photos of his daughter Jennifer, embracing her daughter, Isabel, outside a rustic-looking log cabin in the Rocky Mountains. They both looked scared and there were North Korean armed guards standing around them. The next photo showed Jennifer and Isabel wearing prisoner's outfits, light blue drab outfits with a four-digit number sewn over the breast. They looked to be in a dark, empty room. There was the edge of a toilet visible in the right side of the photo. The last photo was the most haunting of all, for it showed only his granddaughter Isabel in the same room. Jennifer was gone.

"I don't believe you . . . " Robert stammered, unconvinced even by his own voice. *How could they have gotten them? And where was Frank, Jennifer's husband?*

"You will make us an atomic bomb, Dr. Miller," Mr. Yuan replied, "or your daughter Jennifer and granddaughter Isabel will die."

5

SACRIFICE

November 23, 2018, Orbit of Comet 2, Vishnu Spacecraft
Ten days to Lunar Impact

*F*inal Diary Entry, Dr. Nia Rhodes: I am troubled in these final hours of my life. Oh, wait, I have to back up. No one knows I have to die—not even Dr. Miller or Dr. Lahdka or the rest of NASA. But I've gone over it for the past three days and I just don't see any alternative.

Four days ago, when I sent the second of two nuclear missiles to Comet 2 to correct its curvature, something went wrong. The explosions were intended to widen the gaseous jet and realign the comet's trajectory so it hit right in the middle of the Moon, but the missile's thrusters didn't work properly. Instead it rocketed away, missing the comet entirely. What's more, when the other missile hit, it did not widen the jet nearly enough. This is hugely problematic, because we cannot risk the comet nearly missing the Moon or we risk the world ending.

So, I did the math, and it doesn't look good. There are no more IMPs traveling to Comet 2 from Earth—and I have two left on the Vishnu Spacecraft. The energy required to direct Comet 2 to hit the Moon directly and use it as a shield most efficiently, we'll need two—point—two thermonuclear devices to be detonated on the surface of the comet.

Now, you'll probably see our problem: we need another fifth of a nuclear explosion at least to get the comet on target. Now, considering that neither Los Alamos nor Pyongsong have the resources or time to build a new IMP, I've come up with one idea: use the Vishnu spacecraft as the last bomb. Aside from having a reserve of liquid oxygen as fuel, there is also a small nuclear reactor aboard the ship. Gerald Jan designed it specifically for this ship—and it really is amazing that the little guy basically powers everything on board.

If there are any nuclear physicists out there, you might say, "Stop! It won't work! The uranium in your reactor is thirty to ninety times too diluted to cause an explosion! It's not even weapons grade!"

Well, that would be true for a nuclear reactor on Earth, with big smoke stacks, but Gerald had to design a new, small one. So, the one that powers Vishnu does in fact use weapons-grade, scary, big "explosion-style" uranium.

You've probably guessed by now. I have to fly this ship into the comet. I've worked out the modeling. Ugh, it's not going to be fun.

So . . . yeah.

In other news, the billionaires' Ark, which I can see clearly with my telescope, is orbiting along. I wonder if they are worried about colliding with Comet 3, or the debris from the Lunar Impact.

It's possible that their paths could intersect. I'm sure they have been tracking the comet, though. Anyway, they probably have escape pods that are safe. They probably even have Pop-Tarts to eat as they eject themselves *down to Earth, or Snickers bars. I'm so sick of space food.*

. . .

Janice tried to concentrate on her breathing in her tree pose in the exercise room. She brought the heel of her ankle as high as possible against her thigh while placing her hands above her head in prayer formation. At its core, the act of yoga was a task of trying to concentrate on three things at once: calming the mind, slowing the breathing, and balancing the muscles to create the desired stretching pose.

She looked out onto the Milky Way, excited about her decision to take one of the escape hatches. She came to the conclusion to leave for two main reasons. First, she was worried that the fastidious Mr. Kaser would find out that it was her who sent the information to Earth about the bunker in Houston. She also feared what living on the ark would do to her mind—at times, she felt she was going crazy.

As she stood with her eyes closed in tree pose, the problems in her plan listed themselves neatly in her brain. One: the pod bay was password protected, and the launch codes required a fingerprint scan of each individual. Mr. Kaser had made sure that no one could leave on anyone else's pod, of which there were two hundred. Two: each pod would fit two people, but Janice and Alex were each assigned to different pods. Janice would need to reprogram one of the pods to allow both of them to travel. At the moment, she was set to go with her father, so, she would have to reprogram it so that Alex and she could go together. If she went alone, it would mean that at least one person would have to stay behind on the Ark and die in space. As much as she hated the billionaires, she didn't need any more death on her conscience.

Janice was confident that she would be able to shift the required fingerprint from her father's thumb to Alex's, and then switch her father's so that when it came time for him to leave, he would just have to leave with the Russian drilling expert instead of his daughter.

Alex would also have to agree to going on the pod. Janice had the password codes to all of the checkpoints, so they would be able to access food and weapons wherever they landed, in case the GPS system of the pods was faulty.

All in all, it seemed that the team at NASA had done a good job in keeping as many people alive as possible. At night, areas of Earth were illuminated. Moscow, for example, and areas of North Korea, and some pockets in South America as well. Much of the United States was dark, though in the southwest Janice thought she could see a faint light—Los Alamos.

Janice slowly relaxed her leg back down to the ground and flexed her left knee, raising her heel to her groin this time. *As long as Alex agrees, we'll be able to go,* she thought. Janice thought it would be best to eject themselves to a remote location near a checkpoint. It might be dangerous to land near a place with people living on the ground, because those people living on the ground might not feel too kindly toward the people in the Ark, orbiting safely around the Earth while humanity burned below.

According to the atmospheric readings of the Earth, the ozone layer had been greatly depleted. As a result the ultraviolet radiation coming from the Sun went straight through, so people living on the surface would have to shield themselves from the sunlight during the day or risk severe sunburns. Janice shuddered. *Living on Earth will be very different*, she thought.

Janice finished her yoga exercises and walked to the computer work area, where she found Alex.

"So, Alex," she began, sitting next to him, "I was thinking you could switch pods with my father. That way, we wouldn't be leaving anyone behind to die on the Ark and we could still leave early. We could lead our own lives, Alex, away from this corruption forever."

Alex thought for a long time about Janice's

proposition, and it was enough time for another man to come into the computer room to begin working. Alex thought about how close everyone was to leaving the Ark anyway, and how the Earth did in fact seem welcoming—its green-blue hues always visible from their ship. While the man typed away at his keyboard, Alex looked over from his chair at Janice, and said, "Okay, let's do it." He looked wary but altogether like someone rapidly running out of options.

They both smiled at each other, and the man looked up only momentarily from his work when they spoke. They resolved to meet in the computer room in three days to organize their things. For Janice, the three days flew by, and before she knew it, she was back at the computer room, with Alex beside her, both of them ready to finally return to Earth.

Together they worked on switching the thumbprints of the pods so that Janice and Alex could leave together.

"Oh, I didn't tell you," Alex said. "Mr. Kaser came to talk to me a week ago. He wanted to know why I changed the code to those solar panels. I think he suspects me of doing it on purpose. I just think it's good we are leaving. Mr. Kaser demanded answers. He looked fierce, like he wanted to punish me very badly. Even though I didn't do anything wrong, if Mr. Kaser believes I did, he'll act."

"I'm glad we are leaving together," Janice answered, feeling a twinge of guilt.

Finishing the code only took a few hours, and since they didn't need to cover up their tracks, Alex breezed through the brunt of the hacking. Once they were inside the pod and started the engines it would be too late for anyone to stop them. Alex busied himself by going back to his room and grabbing a few keepsakes to bring with him, and to say one final word to his father.

"Don't you want to do the same with your Dad?" Alex asked.

"I have nothing to say to him," Janice responded.

"Come on, Janice," Alex urged. "Listen. Whatever he did that made you so mad at him while you've been on this ship, he still has your best interests at heart. I mean, he did save a place for you on this ship, right? And he's your father; you should say what you need to say. You may never see him again."

Janice groaned, but acknowledged begrudgingly that Alex had a point. She finished the fingerprint switch, and made her way to the room where she knew her father would be. It was near Mr. Kaser's room, and as she suspected, her father Charles was sipping a scotch and reading an old history book. He looked genuinely surprised and excited to see her.

"Janice! I . . . I didn't expect you."

"Hey Dad, how are you?"

"Oh, just fine, honey—just reading."

"Right."

"So, what's up?"

Janice shuffled uncomfortably around before picking a spot on the couch opposite her father's lounge chair.

"I guess I just wanted to say," Janice began, looking down and rubbing her fingers together, "thank you. I know we haven't always seen eye to eye, but you've always done what you thought was best for me, and I respect that. Thank you for bringing me up here. I'm sorry for being so . . . antisocial over the past few months."

Charles looked up from his book and raised his eyebrows. "I would use a different word. Not antisocial but maybe—"

"Dad, listen. I'm trying to apologize," Janice interrupted.

"Right, I'm sorry. Well, thank you then."

Janice nodded, and they sat there a while not knowing what to say to each other. Then, just like that, Janice made an awkward face, pulling her lips into her mouth, and kissed her father on the cheek. She had a feeling it would be the last time she would see her father.

Janice walked down to her bunk, where she looked over her keepsakes to see if she wanted to bring any of them with her, but saw no reason to. She simply grabbed the little bag she had packed and headed down to the stern of the ship—the part closest to the thrusters originally used to eject the ship into space. It was a part of the ship that people often had no reason to go into, but Alex was there waiting for her, nervously biting his fingernails.

"You ready?" Alex asked. He cradled a small suitcase in his arms, which made Janice laugh. The pods barely had room for two full grown adults, let alone a carry-on suitcase.

"What do you have in there?" Janice asked.

"Oh, just some things that are important to me," Alex answered bashfully.

"Alex, you know that won't fit into the pod right?"

Alex looked down at his suitcase and chuckled to himself. "Yeah, I guess so."

So he opened the suitcase, and out spilled a large amount of photos. There were photos of snowy scenes with people standing outside of log cabin houses probably somewhere in Russia. The people wore huge jackets and fur hats with ear flaps and stared solemnly at the camera. Alex picked one of them up and stuffed it into his jacket pocket and then picked up an old watch which he also jammed into a pocket. Then he left the suitcase on the ground.

"Alright, let's go," he said, looking to Janice.

"Let's go," she replied.

They entered the escape pod bay, which had no gravity, and looked at the rows upon rows of escape pods, organized in three levels. To Janice it looked like a room in a *Star Wars* ship, and she pulled herself into the room by the handrails. They floated over to door number thirty-seven—the escape pod they would take. Upon opening the door to the pod, they realized the interior was even smaller than they thought. It had no windows and no cameras, only a screen in front of two seats. Each person was made to wear a spacesuit and most of the pod's thrusters were computerized. All crew members of the Ark had been trained to operate the pods, so they already knew the mechanics. The pods were comprised of three modules, two of which would burn up in the atmosphere, meaning that the bulk of the pod would burn up during their journey.

The twosome got in their spacesuits and settled into their seats and the pod began its systems checks to ensure a successful launch. Janice had some paranoid thoughts that an alarm would sound at them leaving the Ark, but nothing of the sort happened. Janice felt a little as if she was getting ready for a really scary rollercoaster ride, like the ones at Six Flags. When she looked over at Alex, though, his white face looked even more bleached.

"I take it you're nervous," Janice joked.

"Aren't you?" Alex asked, looking anxious. "The flight up was scary enough, but going down? Have you thought of how far we are about to travel—and how fast?"

"Trying not to think about it."

"Easier said than done," Alex responded, trying to do breathing exercises.

After another few minutes, Janice began to sweat inside the spacesuit. Then, finally, the screen in front of her flashed the *Okay*, meaning that the pod was ready for takeoff. Janice was amazed momentarily at how automated the Ark was. Gone were the days of pilots sitting around walls of buttons, pushing tens of them at once to check all their systems. It had simply become one button, and all systems were *Go*.

The pods were programmed to land in the ocean close to a coast, but the pilot had to select which coast based on the current location of the Ark. The pod's navigation system calculated several options for them. Suddenly, a loud buzzing sounded from outside the pod.

"Systems shutdown in ten . . . nine . . . " a voice said inside the pod.

The locations weren't available yet from the calculations, and wouldn't be done in time before the countdown finished.

"Someone must have realized we engaged one of the escape pods," Alex said. "Let's just go. Who cares where we land, right? We're together."

"Okay," Janice answered rapidly, and they kissed quickly before hitting the *Launch* button.

The countdown stopped and the pod began to detach from the Ark. The changes in velocity threw Janice into her harness. It was the first time Janice had felt true claustrophobia. It was unbelievable how small the compartment was. Then Janice imagined, just for a moment, what lay beyond the thick metal walls of their pod for hundreds and hundreds of miles—empty, dangerous, unforgiving space.

The small metal ball thrashed and bounced and rumbled through the atmosphere of the Earth, bringing a new meaning to the phrase, "a bumpy ride." Alex screamed for his life while Janice could think of nothing other than reminding herself to breathe. *In and out and in and out*, she thought. It turned out that all the yoga came in handy, as the breathing exercises calmed her. As the violent descent continued, she reached out to grab Alex's hand.

The automated pilot did most of the work, and a connection with the Ark even told them about where they would land. As they hurtled through the air, Janice found herself trying to focus on the altimeter to tell her how close they were to the Earth, but it was difficult with the tumbling and violent vibrations of the escape pod. The adrenaline coursing through her veins made time impossible to tell.

Finally, there was a large force, which jerked everything straight toward the screen of the pod. The screen cracked. Then, they slowly began traveling upwards again. It took them almost a minute for them to finally stop accelerating, and the escape pod began bobbing up and down. The cracked screen flashed "error" in red. Janice stretched her neck, sore from the impact.

She looked over at Alex, whom she happily noticed was still breathing.

"Are you okay?" she asked.

"I'm alive," he answered breathlessly. "I don't like heights, and I'm never going to space again, but I'm alive."

Finally, the *Door Open* button flashed green, allowing Janice to open the door. The door was directly above them. Janice released the hatch to a bright sky and the smell of the sea. Janice peeked out of the escape pod and saw water. She turned around and breathed out heavily when she saw a coastline several kilometers away.

"Thank God. I thought we had landed in the middle of the ocean," Janice said, relieved.

Alex did not say anything, but wore a big smile. He longed to kiss the sandy beach once they got there.

"Where do you think we are?" Janice wondered.

Along the coast were enormously tall crags, only it looked like they simply stopped at a certain altitude. They went on horizontally for almost ten kilometers. It was a beautiful site, and it lorded over the surrounding land majestically. It looked like it was the home of some ancient gods who did not find a need for their people to build great churches or massive monuments to their power; they did that themselves with this atypical natural wonder.

Perhaps some god had sliced off the top of the mountain. That was what it looked like—as if a god had chopped the mountain off with a sharpened scythe.

Their adventure was not over yet, because they still had to paddle their way to shore. They were a few kilometers out from the beach, with no other way to get there other than to paddle with their hands.

"Where do you think we are?" Janice asked.

"I've been here!" Alex replied. "My father used to take me here on vacation during the frigid Russian winter. We're in Camps Bay, a suburb of Cape Town, South Africa. That crazy-looking flat mountain is called Table Mountain."

It took a few hours to finally get ashore, and by the time they did, their arms and backs ached. The city itself looked desolate and ghostly. It seemed like it had been deserted a long time ago. As Janice moved to get out of the pod, she immediately felt drowsy and weak, being only able to crawl out of the escape pod. Although she had tried to keep her muscles as functional as possible during her time in space, the amount of zero gravity she was forced to live in on the Ark had atrophied her muscles severely.

"So, what now?" Alex asked, breathing heavily.

Janice checked the bunker locations.

"Now, we walk to our new home."

6

IMPACT

December 3, 2018, Cape Town, South Africa
Hours to Comet-Moon Impact

After resting under the awning of an abandoned hotel for a minute, Janice and Alex started toward the nearest bunker location. Janice had brought with her a map of all of the checkpoint locations in the world, and there was one perhaps a day or two's walk away. As they looked out upon the African continent, their energy returned. It was truly beautiful to finally be back on Planet Earth, no longer stuck in the small metal box that was the Ark. The feeling of vastness of the Earth, the smell of real air, and especially the feel of gravity, gave Janice a feeling of joy and happiness she had never felt before.

In the escape pod was a two weeks' supply of food which they carried in backpacks. Janice and Alex were wrapped up in the inner linings of their space-suits to protect themselves from the hot Sun, and Janice felt like she was a character from *Star Wars*, shipwrecked on an alien planet which had been abandoned by its species long ago.

On the previous trip to the area, Alex's father had helped construct a diamond mine in the north-west of the country, and as a vacation he and Alex had visited Cape Town for a weekend. It was a truly beautiful city once, but now it was a dreadful sight. They'd landed in Camps Bay, an affluent beach town suburb of Cape Town, nestled cozily in between the South Atlantic and Table Mountain. To the north of Table Mountain was a small bypass between the actual mountain and a second peak, called Lion's Head. Alex said they should walk in between these two, which would bring them to the bunker checkpoint. Janice's map confirmed this.

Thus, they continued walking north, through the dilapidated architecture of Camps Bay.

• • •

Robert sat in Dr. Kang's office with a tired Mr. Yuan and Dr. Kang. Robert was handcuffed to his chair by his left hand. He tried his best to keep his daughter out of his mind, but it was impossible.

He had just watched in horror the recording—dated two days prior—of the Vishnu spacecraft as it hurtled into Comet 2. The explosion stopped the feed immediately, and Robert used his free hand to replay the recording, watching the ship crash purposefully into Comet 2.

This makes sense why we couldn't contact her yesterday. Dr. Rhodes just sacrificed herself. Why?

The recording had been sent only to Robert, but the North Koreans had kept the video from reaching him. Finally, hours before impact and still unable to understand what the video meant, they wanted to know if they should head underground.

"What does this mean?" a nervous Mr. Yuan asked. "Is Comet 2 going to hit Earth?"

Our models must have been incorrect and the comet needed another blast to stay in line to hit the Moon, or maybe she wanted it all to end, or maybe something went wrong with the ship, Robert thought, wracking his brain for all the reasons why Dr. Rhodes might fly into the comet.

"Well, we'll see in a few hours, but going underground won't matter," Robert answered. "The size of this comet will destroy us all, no matter how far we bury ourselves under the surface of the Earth."

I can't believe they kept this from me, Robert thought.

"I need you to take me to the largest telescope you have in Pyongsong," Robert said. "We need to look at the Moon and see if it will successfully block Comet 2. We know Comet 3 will land somewhere in the South Atlantic, and it's smaller, so it should not be a problem."

Within a half an hour they were ten minutes away, looking at a live, high-resolution image of the Moon.

The telescope wasn't powerful enough to track Comet 2, so they simply trained it on the Moon and waited. Robert was un-handcuffed now, with Major Winter beside him. The telescope's images were projected onto a screen as a series of photos, spaced a few seconds apart. The first hundred or so only showed the same Moon, woefully unaware that it was about to take a huge ball of ice and rock to its gut.

While Robert watched the still photos of the Moon before the comet hit it, he hypothesized on what would make Dr. Rhodes do such a disastrous thing as fly into the comet with her ship.

Could she have killed herself? Perhaps she simply let go? No, there must have been a reason for this. She collided with the same spot where we targeted our IMPs.

But that would mean that she would have sacrificed herself, and maybe used the Vishnu spacecraft as a bomb? But that means that the data she sent to us—which showed the comet was on track—must have been doctored. Or maybe she just found out first, realizing there were no other options . . .

Robert was stopped from his musings when the screen showed a tremendous collision and a flash of light so bright that if it was night it would have been visible to the naked eye.

It worked! Robert thought, whooping and jumping into the air. The image of a bright spot on the Moon where the comet hit seemed to glow.

All around him people were cheering and laughing, and Major Winter hugged Robert tightly. "You did it, Robert!" he yelled.

Mr. Yuan hugged Robert too, thanking him profusely. Robert's thoughts about Dr. Rhodes left him then for the moment, an overwhelming relief washed over him. His heart slowed its beat so drastically that

Robert had to sit down, breathing in and out heavily. *It's over,* he thought. *It's really over.*

He felt all the countless sleepless nights catching up to him, all that time spent poring over the data, and all the lives already lost to the effort. Suddenly, he started to weep. The victory for the human race was not televised, or radioed, or even telegrammed around the world—not yet. But for Robert, all that he cared about was that it was finally over. Thankfully, the North Koreans let him return to his cell, where he fell quickly into a deep sleep.

• • •

Robert woke up in a cold sweat to a knock on his door.

"Dr. Miller? Please come with us. NASA is on the line," Mr. Yuan called.

"Okay, give me a minute," Robert said. He looked at his watch. *Only one hour of sleep,* he thought, grimacing. He rubbed his eyes and remembered with dismay that saving the Earth was no longer his only problem.

I need to find a way to save my daughter.

Five minutes later, Robert sat in a conference room with Suri Lahdka on the line, along with the rest of her team, President Chaplin, and Secretary Brighton. Robert half-listened to the congratulations and the celebrations coming from the United States, until Suri brought up Dr. Rhodes's death.

"I had been sent an encrypted email from Dr. Rhodes before she died, and I couldn't figure out what it was or how to open it. It turns out it was a time-dependent email, and I was allowed to open it after the Lunar Impact. Dr. Rhodes calculated that Comet 2's impact trajectory with the Moon was slightly off course, and in realizing that the fate of humanity was at stake, she turned the Vishnu spacecraft into a bomb and used it to correct the comet's path. Dr. Rhodes sacrificed her life for the sake of Planet Earth."

No one spoke for a long minute.

"It's because of her that we are all alive," Robert added. He couldn't keep his mind off his daughter. *What could he do to save her? Where was she?* He remembered the soldiers' stern faces. *Would they bring Jennifer and Isabel here?*

Major Winter had not been imprisoned like Robert. They had told him that Robert was staying at the Pyongsong facility to be closer to his work. Major Winter, though, sensed that something was wrong. The North Koreans were all looking at Robert in a stern, almost condescending way, and he wondered why Robert seemed so detached. All the scientists should be leaping out of their chairs in glory, with Robert as their hero.

"Are you all right, Robert?" Major Winter asked.

"I'm fine," Robert said. He addressed the North Korean scientists. "You've all done tremendous work, each one of you. You should all be very proud." Everyone clapped again happily.

Then everyone turned their attention to Suri on the phone, who had stated that Comet 3 would land in the South Atlantic Ocean in around seventy minutes. Its impact would create severe damage, but only locally. People living within five kilometers of the predicted impact site had hopefully heard the radio message broadcasted by the U.S. government to go to high ground. The U.S. government did not have communications with South America or Africa, so they were on their own in terms of preparing for the tsunami brought on by the comet's impact.

All of this was on Robert's mind as he tried to stop thinking about his daughter, and once Suri hung up, Robert began speaking to Mr. Yuan in a hushed tone.

"Please follow me," Mr. Yuan said.

"Wait!" Major Winter called. "Robert, I need to speak with you."

But the North Korean guards wouldn't have it, and they were separated. *What now?* Robert wondered. Robert was taken to an interrogation room.

After ten minutes of nervously twiddling his thumbs, a guard stepped into the room leading a figure with a black bag over her head. Mr. Yuan removed the bag and Robert breathed in relief at the sight of his frightened daughter. Though she did look terrified and shaken, she was physically unharmed.

"Dad!? Oh my God!" she said with tears running down her face.

Robert ran to hug her, and they grabbed each other tightly.

"What's happening?" Jennifer asked, wiping her eyes. "They separated Isabel and me and took me here. What do they want from us?"

Robert composed himself, wiping a tear from his eye. "They want me to help them build a nuclear bomb for North Korea. They threatened me, Jennifer. They said that if I don't build a nuclear weapon for them, they'll kill you and Isabel."

"Can you—" Jennifer began, but then her voice caught and she began crying again.

"I don't know nearly enough about the practicalities of nuclear fission to build a bomb." Robert eyed Mr. Yuan, who was staring at something in the hallway. "I've explained that to them but they don't seem to care."

"So what do you think will happen?" she asked, grabbing her father's hands.

Robert thought at first this was simply a loving gesture, but realized with intrigue that she shoved something into the palm of his hand. A small piece of paper.

"I wrote it as they took me here," she explained in a whisper. "I stole a pen and paper. They didn't see. I hope you can read it."

"It'll be fine, but watch out. I think they could be listening to us right now. I guess they are letting us meet because they want me to be sure they aren't bluffing—"

Suddenly the door to the hallway opened and in walked one of the government workers—the same one who always seemed to be present when Robert worked. Robert was sure he reported on his progress to Kim Ha Lee. He was clean shaven, wore glasses and a suit, and had a permanent scowl across his face. The man walked over to the corner of the room, folded his arms across his chest, and watched the father and daughter.

"You're okay, though?" Robert asked, hiding the piece of paper in his hands.

"Yes," Jennifer said, looking apprehensively toward the dark corner where the government official stood.

"And Isabel? Is she okay, too?"

"Yes, we are fine. I'm, um, looking forward to you finishing your work here, so we can all go back home."

"Me too, my sweet daughter, me too," Robert agreed, hugging his daughter again and hoping that they were both thinking the same thing: *I'm going to get you out of here; we are going to escape here somehow, someway . . .*

When he got back to his cell, he went into the bathroom where he figured there would be no cameras, and looked at the piece of paper crumpled up in his hands.

154 steps left, 120 steps right, 73 steps left, up thirteen stairs . . .

The writing, which was incredibly messy, must have been done while Jennifer walked through the enormous building in Pyongsong, from her holding cell to the room where they met.

7

IRONY

Later That Day, Los Alamos, New Mexico

Suri got off the phone with Robert, leaving her with Dr. Ivanov and the other scientists who sat in the conference room, re-watching the images that North Korea had sent them. She sat apprehensively watching the Moon in its majesty. The second head of the three-headed monster had simply vanished—as if the Moon ate it up. As it crashed, the Moon's surface material rocketed into space. From the photos it looked like the Moon's rock acted much like water when a stone is thrown into it. The water depresses initially, and then shoots upwards from the force of the impact, and then the shock waves extend outward until equilibrium is found once again.

"Amazing," Dr. Ivanov gasped, "Three years and countless dead, but ve did it. Ve saved ze Earth from almost complete destruction."

Suri agreed by nodding. Then, when the next photo came up, she saw something curious. She immediately spoke up.

"That light," she began, "in the bottom right corner. What is that? There's a small illumination."

"Perhaps two of the debris particles collided together?" Dr. Ivanov offered.

"I don't know; they would need a lot of energy to produce that much light, and their trajectory does not support a collision."

"Maybe they collided with remnants of a satellite," Dr. Ivanov said, uninterested, still thinking about their accomplishments.

Suri kept looking until the next photo appeared, showing a larger flash in the same location as the flash before, and again she wondered what it could have been. *What did the debris hit?* she wondered. Then, like the feeling of finally getting a math problem right after staring at it forever, the light bulb went off in her head.

Suri gasped.

"Expand on that area of space, as much as you can," she said.

Suri held her breath as Dr. Ivanov zoomed in.

Suri did not respond, and Dr. Ivanov squinted at the photos, also unable to decipher what the small flicker of light could mean. When the next photo came and they zoomed in, they could actually see that it was not one small dot, but instead many dots, all lit, and moving toward Earth! It was with dread that her preliminary hypothesis was confirmed.

"It's the billionaire's Ark," she whispered.

"But that doesn't explain the many light points. Are you sure?" Dr. Ivanov replied doubtfully.

"The light points could be escape pods," Suri said.

"Could they be pieces of the ship?" Dr. Ivanov asked.

"Hmmm," Suri said, watching as Dr. Ivanov magnified the photos. Streaks of light were connected to the light points.

"You're right," Dr. Ivanov said. "They're escape pods. My God."

Suri counted fifteen of the pods successfully escaping. She refocused on the midst of the debris, but couldn't spot the billionaire's Ark anymore. There was too much debris in space to make it out.

Suri watched sadly as only sixteen space pods made their way toward Earth. Judging by the size of the escape pods, they could only hold one or two people at most.

Suri sat back in her chair, rubbing her temples and her eyebrows. She remembered back, more than a year ago, hearing that a group of billionaire businessmen and aristocrats had built an Ark that would launch into space and orbit until the threat of the comet passed. She remembered that they had even elicited the help of a terrorist to bomb her airplane, because they had actually supported the idea of drastically reducing the population of the Earth. Now, they had gotten their wish—half of the population of the Earth *was* gone. However, now most of the billionaires were gone, too. *A sad irony,* she thought.

To her right she saw Dr. Ivanov crying silently.

"Did you know someone on the Ark?" Suri asked tenderly.

Dr. Ivanov looked over to Suri then around to the other scientists. Suri thought that he was looking to make sure there were no government officials listening in on them. When he saw no one, he said, "My cousin and uncle. Alexander and Nikita Chekhov."

"I'm so sorry for your loss," Suri said sincerely.

Dr. Ivanov nodded solemnly.

8

GOD'S WILL

December 4, 2018: Somewhere near Cape Town, South Africa
Day One Post-Lunar Impact

Janice and Alex ate from their nutrition packs as they walked slowly along the M62 highway toward the bunker. They were both incredibly weak and needed frequent breaks. Janice knew they were lucky; when astronauts lived in space for months at a time, they would return to Earth ostensibly in a wheelchair.

"Do you think the comet landed already? Maybe it even burned up in the atmosphere," Alex mused.

"It was too large to burn up, Alex."

They were both thirsty and tired, but Janice found solace in the beautiful view, because even though it was bereft of trees and vegetation, the ocean looked beautiful and the peak of Lion's Head was impressive, rising up thousands of feet above them.

They continued walking along the road toward Vredehoek—the location of the bunker—when they decided to take a break next to a large boulder. They leaned on it, drinking water. Then suddenly, a red glow appeared in the west, over the ocean.

"What's that?" Alex wondered.

"Oh, no," Janice said dejectedly. "I think it means that the comet must have hit in the Atlantic."

Alex swore.

God, how unlucky are we? Janice thought.

"What should we do?" Alex asked.

Then, without warning, the ground moved suddenly and knocked them both off their feet. The rumbling continued as they tried to steady themselves.

"We need to get as high as possible," Janice said as she tried to steady herself on the boulder next to her. "It hit in the ocean; that means a tsunami is going to come here."

The ground shock died down after another minute, and they began climbing up Lion's Head as fast as they could. Janice looked back at the ocean, but the water did not recede like she thought it would. Both Janice and Alex were sweating profusely from hiking. Suddenly, a deafening sound—a loud deep rumble—hit their ears. The sound was accompanied by a large wind blast which knocked the twosome off their feet again.

"Come on!" Alex yelled, over the cacophony. "We need to go up!"

Alex pulled up Janice and together they struggled upwards again. Janice pushed herself to climb, even crawling up the side of the mountain at times. Her knees were bloody and her fingers were sore from scratching at the ground.

"We are in a valley, Janice, it's no use!" Alex moaned from behind her.

"We have to try! We have to," Janice breathed.

But Janice felt in her heart that Alex was right. As she looked back toward the ocean, she saw an impossible sight. A wall of water hundreds of feet high was rushing toward them at an incredible pace. Janice realized with dread that there was only one place for it to go.

This was no normal tsunami; this was a megatsunami, only created by large amounts of mass falling into large bodies of water. The height of the column of water raised at an impossible height, and it steamrolled onto the land, picking up the sides of buildings, dead trees, cars, everything, quicker than Janice thought possible. Alex called behind her.

"It's time!" he yelled over the sound of the gargantuan wave rapidly approaching.

Janice looked back to the man she had convinced to take a chance and return to Earth with her, and felt a tear fall from her cheek. The water was so loud she could not hear Alex anymore. She crawled back down to him.

"I love you," he said, but Janice couldn't hear him.

Janice felt confused and scared and grabbed Alex's hands.

"I love you," she mouthed at him, kissing him hard on the mouth.

They held each other close as the water filled the valley and rushed toward them. Then the water came higher. It engulfed them completely, the power of the ocean raging past them as if they weren't even there . . .

● ● ●

One day post-impact, and it was hard to imagine for Jeremy, but it was true: for three years the world was consumed with the daunting task of stopping the comet from destroying all life on Earth, and although the comet had devastated the planet, humanity had endured.

Now Jeremy found himself living in Los Alamos

among the most important people in the govern-ment. These same people were currently locked in the largest conference room at the National Laboratory complex, discussing the next step for the United States of America. Jeremy sat with Anna, Dustin, and Karina in the lobby, waiting for what they would say.

"I think they should have let us in, even if we weren't going to be allowed to speak," Karina said.

Jeremy agreed, "Yeah, it would have been nice, but I also understand why they didn't."

"We're basically kids in their eyes. If I was their age I'm not sure I'd want to hear my own advice," Anna offered.

"We may be kids in age, but certainly not in experience. We lived through a time when millions, probably even billions, of people died, and we made it out the other side. If we can do that we should be able to at least listen to how the United States will shape the New World Order."

"I think we should acknowledge how lucky we

are," Dustin reminded everyone. "I mean, from you guys living in the mansion with the military guys, to us traveling to Israel and living for a month in an Israeli bunker, it's clear that we were pretty fortunate to come out of this alive."

"Anna actually came out of it pregnant! So alive twice, in a sense," Karina joked, and everyone laughed.

Then, suddenly and without warning, Jeremy's own laughter turned hysterical, then finally to a solemn sob. He cried because of all the death that hung in the world's atmosphere, from the starvation that was sure to kill a lot more in the coming years, and from the utter and drastic change of everything he held dear. The others, initially shocked by Jeremy's change of emotion, became overcome with sorrow, and joined him in a teary embrace.

Sometimes you just need to cry it out.

• • •

Suri sat in the large conference room listening to Secretary Brighton and President Chaplin outline their proposal for governance in the United States. Suri tried to listen as well as she could but she still felt a little dazed from all that had happened. It was hard for her to even think about the future.

Everything was so uncertain. When it came to her old job—tracking down comets in the Kuiper Belt for research purposes—well, she wouldn't be able to get back to doing that anytime soon. The satellites that she needed weren't functioning anymore, as the debris from the lunar impact had destroyed many of them. Not to mention the world had *much* more pressing issues to deal with. Suri tuned back in to the meeting when she heard something about Robert, and realized that it was President Chaplin speaking:

"Now is the time for us to rebuild. The United States of America is now completely separated through unforeseen and unparalleled forces of nature. Nothing that we could have predicted or done could have prepared us for what we must accomplish now. We have been living in an anarchy caused by the very real fear that the world was going to end. By the grace of God and our brilliant team of scientists, led by Dr. Robert Miller and Dr. Suri Lahdka, our world has been saved and the United States will prevail. The world is in disarray, and many people have died, but we must re-establish control.

"As President of the United States, I propose we begin by rebuilding this world in a new way, with a new outlook, and that begins with having an understanding of the survivors in our country. Immediately we must begin planting crops, and the delivery of the seeds from the Svalbard Global Seed Vault will help us achieve this vision.

"I want to send teams of soldiers around the United States to gather a census. We need to get an accurate depiction of how many people have survived. Those teams going to Seattle, Minnesota, Vermont, and other states bordering Canada will venture above and make contact with the Canadian government. Those going to states bordering Mexico will have the same objective. Oh, and we will make sure to assign soldiers to their home states. Tensions will be high in these areas, so be careful. Many people still believe that: a) the government does not exist anymore, and b) we could be seen as attackers. Therefore it's important we seem as non-threatening as possible. Is that understood?"

As President Chaplin finished her monologue, Secretary Brighton nodded, along with General Diaz, who led what was left of the armed forces. Suri had been offered the position—with Dr. Miller, when he returned—of rebuilding NASA's telescopes.

"Your leadership and willingness to take calculated risks in deterring the comet show you have the capacity to make difficult decisions under pressure," President Chaplin praised Suri.

Suri thanked the president, and then General Diaz coughed in order to get the attention of the room.

"Well, there is one issue I do think we need to

address," the general began, "and that is the matter of your tenure, Madam President. You have exceeded your term limit. We need to have an election to determine the next president."

The room sat, a little shocked at the general's comment. Then, Secretary Brighton answered the military man.

"While I agree that we must preserve the integrity of our Constitution and our nation, General Diaz, right now is really not the time. We have no idea how many people are even still alive in the United States. It could be upwards of a hundred million people, or about a third of our population. Surely you understand that there are more important things to accomplish right now aside from an election."

President Chaplin added, addressing the entire room, "I also would like to say that once we have secured the stability of our country, once we have secured food for those alive, and once we have returned our country to a *United* States of America—with a functioning Congress and Judiciary—I will fully resign as president."

General Diaz looked as though he did not like this answer to his motion for an election. He looked to have a lot more to say on the subject, but as he surveyed the room he could see that nearly every person in the room agreed with President Chaplin, so he found it pointless to object.

"General, would you like to begin your presentation?" Secretary Brighton asked.

"Yes. Thank you, Mr. Secretary," General Diaz said, shuffling around some papers and shifting his attention. "I have made contact with North Korea, and they are thus far unresponsive as to repatriating Dr. Robert Miller or Major Anton Winter to the United States. I will try again to communicate with them, but I believe that they just aren't answering."

"Do you think they could be holding them hostage?" Suri asked.

General Diaz, always critical of bringing the younger Suri into meetings concerning national security, refused to answer her directly. Instead, he spoke to the entire room purposefully. "We suspect they may be holding them hostage, but think we should make contact with them again to determine Dr. Miller and Major Winter's exact predicaments."

"Very well," President Chaplin sighed, noticing Suri getting snubbed. "Go on."

"As far as surviving nations, we know that Moscow had a vast underground railway network under its city which would feasibly allow for upwards of twenty million people to live while the comets struck. Despite Russia's close proximity to the first impact site, it is likely that many of its citizens have survived within these tunnels. Similarly, China has a massive underground network. North Korea, as we already know, has survived.

"We suspect the entire continent of Africa will succumb to starvation."

That's not new . . . Suri thought with dismay, and General Diaz continued, "We lost contact with Australia, so we have no knowledge of their current status. Japan is destroyed. Much of the population of India has lost their lives, but many of the elite in the large cities were protected. If our own country is any indicator, starvation is rampant among the entire world, and as of now that should be our primary concern—growing as much food as we possibly can.

"Our analysts estimate that in three years, at least half of the population on the Earth will be gone. Dr. Ivanov, would you like to talk to us about the global climate?"

Suri gulped, imagining her parents in India. She wiped tears from her eyes.

Dr. Ivanov wearily looked at the exhausted individuals gathered around the table. It would take an immense amount of work to return things to normal, if in fact normalcy returned at all.

"Vell, our tests conclude that ze ozone layer has been reduced by almost seventy-five percent. It remains to be seen if these UV-B resistant plants will grow, much less if they will feed ze population. Ve must see. Earth is still ze only habitable planet in ze solar system, though much of our water has been contaminated by acid and black rain. Fortunately, most underwater wells and stored reservoirs avoided contamination. Also, for better or worse, there are a lot fewer living humans, so providing everyone with drinking water will be an easier problem."

"Is there a projection on how long it will take for the ozone layer to return to its original state?" President Chaplin asked, taking notes.

"At the current moment, no, ve need many more data points. However, ze Earth, like any ecosystem, has a tendency to return back to equilibrium, so ve may just have to wait and see how quickly that happens. There is also the matter of volcanic activity. Ze impacts have catalyzed many volcanic eruptions that have spewed large amounts of sulfur dioxide and other gases, which are toxic if inhaled.

"From all this despair though, there is a silver lining. Ze human activity that has been contributing to ze global climate change has disappeared. Without the refineries, toxic chemical plants, and poisonous plastics polluting our air and environment, ze Earth might recover more quickly than ve think. Maybe this is a strike from God."

The room stopped then, and everyone looked over to Dr. Ivanov.

"Did you just say that God caused this comet strike?" President Chaplin asked in disbelief.

"No, I just said it was possible. A way to think about it, if it makes you feel better," Dr. Ivanov said, and then asked suddenly, "Madam President, are you a Christian?"

"I . . . was," President Chaplin stammered, unsure of how to answer the question. She hadn't thought about Christianity in a long time.

"Vell, I am Russian Orthodox. I don't believe in ze Bible literally, but perhaps some events happen by 'God's will'—or whatever you want to call it. Ze story of Noah's Ark bears a strong resemblance to this, does it not? Maybe ve aren't on a boat, and maybe there aren't two of each animal left on Earth, but it does seem like something was unhappy with what was happening on ze Earth, and wanted to start anew. Now, half ze world's population is dead, and ze Earth is repairing itself. Maybe ve can now learn from our mistakes of ze nineteenth and twentieth centuries? Maybe ve can have a more evolved, civilized world where ve respect both land, person and everything around us? Maybe this new world is God's will."

The group sat in silence for a second as Dr. Ivanov returned his gaze to the papers in front of him. Everyone looked around uncomfortably, and Suri shook her head. *God's will that half the population died?* Dr. Ivanov had spoken so aloofly, half-expecting his audience to dismiss him in a fit of laughter. But the meeting went on as if he had never spoken, though there wasn't a person in that room that didn't glance up at the ceiling, wondering if what he said was true.

9

PREY

December 17, 2018, Pyongsong Launch Facility, North Korea
Day Fourteen Post-Impact

Robert sat in his holding cell in Pyongsong, hunched over the piece of paper that his daughter had given him. Major Winter sat next to him, also hunched over. In the days after the comet, Major Winter had been placed into an adjoining holding cell, because Robert had told the North Koreans that they needed to collaborate on their knowledge in order to build the North Koreans a workable nuclear bomb.

They now sat bent over the desk in such a way that the video camera wouldn't be able to see what they were writing. They did this to ensure the North

Koreans wouldn't listen in on their conversation, and so they wrote to each other on a small piece of paper.

I'll die before I help give away any secrets, Major Winter wrote.

I know. Me too.

What's your plan?

I have to get Jennifer and Isabel out of here, Robert Miller wrote. *I can't stall much longer about teaching them. I'm even trying to learn about the process of nuclear bombs, but from their books and resources it would take me at least ten years to build something remotely capable of explosion . . . I think escaping is the best choice we have. Are you with me?*

Yes, but she's probably in a cell or something. Are you sure she's still here, in the same building?

Mr. Yuan said he would allow me to see her again today. He said as long as I promise to make them a bomb, I can see her as much as I want. So, what do you think?

Major Winter stared at Robert directly in the eyes and nodded solemnly.

You know what this means? It's very possible we'll die, Robert wrote.

Better than working in a North Korean labor camp for the rest of our lives. They weren't going to let us go anyway.

Memorize the location, then, and we'll go.

Remember our plan, Major Winter wrote. *We have to follow it exactly for it to work. Now, eat the paper. You half and me half.*

Their plan might be unsuccessful, but he had to try. Robert was tired. He felt like in the past three years he'd aged more than the previous fifty. He bet that President Chaplin and Secretary Brighton felt the same way. He had saved the world, twice, and now North Korea wanted him to help build a nuclear weapon. Life around the age of retirement sure didn't feel like a vacation, but pitying himself at this point wouldn't do any good. He knew what he had to do.

Robert looked up from the little note-writing session and regretfully crumpled up the paper, ripped it in half, and started to chew on his piece. The paper quickly clumped in his mouth and the ink bled and mixed with his saliva—a revolting taste. He soldiered on until he could swallow the little ball of paper.

It was time.

Just then Mr. Yuan walked into his room. *Phew*, he thought as Mr. Yuan led them to his office.

As they walked, Mr. Yuan tried to converse with Robert but he wasn't in the mood. Despite being on opposite sides in life, Robert liked Mr. Yuan. There was something about the way that Mr. Yuan spoke and acted, but Robert couldn't quite place it. Sometimes it felt like Mr. Yuan felt guilty about and sympathized with Robert, and that he secretly hated living under an authoritarian regime. Robert had to remind himself that the regime didn't just start with the comet—Mr. Yuan had lived in a fascist state his entire life.

Mr. Yuan smiled before leaving Robert and Major Winter in a small room. They were surrounded by large stacks of books, all on the topic of nuclear physics. The funny thing was, with the information about nuclear physics, building a design for a weapon was not all that difficult. Simply put: all Robert had to do was get enough radioactive material to a "critical mass," throw it together with a conventional explosive, and a chain reaction would create a nuclear explosion.

The hard part, however, was getting the isotopes of uranium or plutonium that are fissile, which meant their nuclei could break apart relatively easily. Plutonium was one of the most toxic chemicals known to humans, making it very difficult to work with, and almost impossible to find in nature. *Though actually, maybe there is some at the impact location*, Robert mused.

Robert shook himself from his reverie to prepare mentally for his plan. *You're not building them a bomb, no matter how intellectually stimulating it might be*, he chided himself.

Robert waited until just before lunch to initiate their plan. Both Robert and the major walked down the hallway toward a small room where both of them were allowed to go. Just one guard was stationed outside their door, nodding to them as they motioned to go in. This room was a sort of makeshift library, which had all the information about nuclear weapons manufacturing available to the North Koreans. Robert and Major Winter were allowed to go in there to take books back to their office. This library was also on the way to Jennifer's cell, or at least where she was hopefully still being held.

Fortunately there was no one else in the room when Robert and Major Winter walked in. Together they went over their plan verbally one more time, counted to three, and began.

Major Winter opened the door a crack, and looked at the guard, who nodded absentmindedly at the major. There was no one else in the hallway. Major Winter, faster than anyone his age, swiftly grabbed the guard by the neck, being sure to cover his mouth. He muffled the guard's scream just in time.

Then Major Winter, using the knife the guard held on his belt, cut the man's throat. He grabbed the guard's utility belt and put it on, then grabbed the machine gun and the security keys to open the doors around the building. After dragging the guard's body down to the back corner of the room, they moved a bookcase to obstruct the view of the body from the door. Any extra second they had before the entire country knew they were fugitives would be valuable.

Robert looked sadly at the pile of elementary physics books and pulled the pistol from the man's belt.

"Remember, the last resort should be using the guns. Once we use them, the entire building will come toward the noise and we'll be overrun. And just follow my lead," Major Winter advised.

Robert nodded. Major Winter put on the shoulder strap to the machine gun and hid it on his back under his jacket, and Robert stuck the gun in the back of his waistband. Aside from Robert's nervous facial expression, they looked like they just might be innocently lost in the large building. Robert was expected to meet Mr. Yuan in his office in one hour to see Jennifer, so they had a little over an hour before they would be identified as missing. Major Winter cracked open the door to the hallway.

There was no one in the hallway. They ran outside and Major Winter walked in the direction that Jennifer's map led them. Twice they heard footsteps approaching and used the keycard stolen from the guard to duck into supply closets. They were fortunate to remain undetected, and then they reached the elevator.

They exhaled in relief when it opened—empty. Jennifer's map told them she waited in the elevator for thirty-four seconds, going up. So, they reversed her route, and Major Winter pushed the button for twelve floors below their current floor. Robert looked at his watch.

Major Winter prayed no one in between the floors hit the button signaling the elevator to stop.

Twenty-one, twenty-two . . . twenty-six, twenty -seven, Robert counted. Whatever floor they passed at thirty—four seconds was Jennifer's.

Bingo, Robert thought, as they rode past the tenth floor.

"She's on the tenth floor," Robert said, but didn't depress the button fast enough, so they went down one extra floor, to nine.

Major Winter made to point his gun at the door as it opened in case there was someone waiting for them on the other side, but Robert told him to hide it.

The door opened and a scientist appeared, entering the elevator. *Damn,* Robert thought, *just our luck.* Robert and Major Winter looked at each other and back at the scientist, tall for a Korean, who eyed them curiously. The scientist hit the button for the fourth floor.

The scientist continued to look oddly at Robert because they didn't exit the elevator.

"We went up one too many," Robert explained nervously to Major Winter.

"No English," the scientist responded.

"Good," Robert replied.

The scientist continued to eye them warily. When he reached in his pocket for his phone, Major Winter decided to act. He knocked the man unconscious with a swift elbow to the temple. Major Winter caught the slumping man and put him down gently on the ground of the elevator just as the elevator *dinged*, signaling that they had reached the fourth floor. Robert stabbed at the elevator button for the tenth floor and the doors shut.

"What should we do with him?" Major Winter asked frantically as the elevator rose upward.

Robert stared ahead, thinking as fast as he could, as the elevator door slowly opened. Robert prayed no one would be waiting for the elevator on the other side. This time, Robert held his pistol out as the door opened. *I really hope I don't have to pull the trigger*, he thought, grimacing.

But this time there was no one waiting. Robert noticed a door leading to the stairway, and decided to place the body of the unconscious scientist there.

Once that was taken care of, Robert and Major Winter continued down the hallway, following Jennifer's instructions.

They made their way through two double doors and past two security guards. They looked sideways at the two, but since Robert was known in the area as the man who had helped save the world from another comet attack, the guards did nothing as the door closed behind them.

"Do you think they'll tell someone?" Major Winter whispered.

"I don't know, maybe they'll talk to Mr. Yuan, which would be bad. He'll probably be looking for us soon. We need to hurry up."

They ran down, left and right, until finally they came to a small dark door flanked by two guards with automatic weapons. Major Winter grabbed

Robert by the arm and dragged him around the corner before they became visible to the guards.

"Do you think that's the room?" Robert asked.

"If you trust Jennifer's instructions, that should be it."

"Let's do it."

There was no one else in the hallway besides the two guards. Together they counted to three and turned around, and before Robert could even draw his pistol, Major Winter had shot both of the guards. They fell in a heap on the floor.

Robert sprinted ahead and over the bodies, and unlocked the door with the keycard. It opened and Jennifer and little seven-year-old Isabel sat together in a corner of the room, hugging each other.

"Dad?!" Jennifer exclaimed.

Robert ran in to console his family while Major Winter dragged the two bodies inside. Isabel screamed when she saw what Major Winter dragged into their room.

Robert went to her. "Shh, it's going to be okay, I promise."

"It's going to be okay, honey," Jennifer said to her daughter. *Someone will have heard Isabel scream,* Robert thought.

Major Winter grabbed the gun of one of the guards and handed it to Jennifer, explaining to her how to use it.

"My husband was a hunter. I know how to use one of these," she said emotionlessly.

Robert remembered meeting her husband Frank a few years prior, just when he'd learned about the incoming comet.

"Is Frank . . . ?" Robert asked, unable to finish the sentence.

"They killed him," Jennifer said resentfully.

"It's time to go," Major Winter called, peeking through a crack in the door to the hallway. Together they ran toward the elevator. As they pressed the down button, they saw far off a few guards running toward them, yelling in Korean.

Major Winter pointed to the stairwell to their right. "Let's go."

They all followed Major Winter's orders. Isabel ran quickly to keep up with Mom, Grandpa Robert, and Major Winter, who was firing at the guards chasing them.

They ran down two stairwells, Robert in front, thinking he was insane to have tried this. They continued down the stairs until suddenly, without warning the door opened and a man walked into the staircase. It happened so abruptly that Robert couldn't avoid running into the man, landing on top of him. The man was none other than Mr. Yuan. Robert quickly got up and helped Mr. Yuan to his feet.

"Whoa, whoa, whoa," Robert said, as Major Winter took aim at the man's head.

"What are you doing, Robert? You're going to get yourself killed," Mr. Yuan looked panicked.

"Wait, Major," Robert said, holding up his palm to Major Winter.

"We know the airfield is not far from here. Drive us to it," Robert said.

"I don't have a car," Mr. Yuan protested.

"Robert, watch the top of the staircase. Jennifer, watch Mr. Yuan," Major Winter ordered, and opened the emergency exit door at the bottom of the staircase. It was a parking garage!

Immediately, the alarm bells sounded and a red light began to flash on and off in the staircase. Isabel began to cry. Robert looked nervously at the staircase above him, thinking he had gotten himself into something that surely would not have a happy ending for anyone. The group followed Major Winter down to the emergency exit, Jennifer training the weapon on Mr. Yuan. Major Winter disappeared through the exit to look for a way out.

They sat there in nervous silence until they heard footsteps and angry Korean being spoken a few floors above them.

"Mr. Yuan," Robert began, "I'm afraid you don't

have a choice. You either help us, or my daughter here will make sure you never see your wife again."

Mr. Yuan looked horrified, and he fingered his wedding ring nervously. He didn't say anything.

Jennifer cocked the hammer of her pistol, and aimed it at Mr. Yuan's forehead.

"They're getting closer," Isabel warned.

Suddenly, a few shots sounded in the parking garage. Then, car tires screeched.

"Come on!" Major Winter's voice called from the exit.

Robert carried Isabel quickly out of the door and into a black SUV.

"He's not moving!" Jennifer called, talking about Mr. Yuan.

"We need to go, now!" Major Winter called from the driver's seat.

Jennifer stuck the barrel of the gun into Mr. Yuan's neck and forced him into the passenger's seat, and she got into the seat behind him, aiming the gun at his temple. Major Winter put the pedal to the metal just as the guards burst through the emergency door, firing bullets into the back of the SUV.

"I'm sorry about this, Mr. Yuan," Robert said, "but we need you to tell us the quickest way to get to the airfield. If you do what we tell you, we'll let you go."

"You don't know what you've done," Mr. Yuan croaked. "They'll kill us all. I'm no hostage—I'm an enemy of the state now."

Despite this, he did point down the road, giving Major Winter directions. Major Winter sped down the road between Pyongsong and Pyongyang and he noticed military vehicles following half a mile behind him.

Mr. Yuan looked sadly behind the car, where six cars were now following them. He wondered when they would start shooting. Mr. Yuan continued to look outside as the cars came closer.

Suddenly Major Winter saw a blockade in front of him, complete with two large SUVs and a police spike strip in between them. Luckily Major Winter took the exit just before the blockade.

"Mr. Yuan," Major Winter said. "We could really use your navigational skills right about now."

"Left here," Mr. Yuan muttered.

Then, speaking more confidently with each direction he gave, Mr. Yuan led then through the backstreets of Pyongyang.

Finally Robert saw what he was hoping for, which was a small wire fence in front of a large field of grass with small strips of concrete—an airfield.

Major Winter saw it too, and drove right through the chain-link fence, which gave way easily. Whatever remnants of the existing plan when they took Jennifer and Isabel from captivity were now flung to the wayside. Their new plan, simply put, was to find a plane and get the hell out of North Korea.

As they drove over the damp grass they could see planes, but apparently the alarms had been sounded, because they also saw soldiers readying guns, and SUVs were turning toward them.

"Mr. Yuan, we need a plane! A cargo plane would be best," Major Winter grunted, unsure of where to steer the car. He swung the vehicle sharply to the right and made to outflank the oncoming assailants.

"Sweetie," Jennifer said, "I want you to get down to the floor and cover your ears, then come up when I tap your back twice. Can you do that for me?"

Isabel nodded rapidly and ducked while Robert and Jennifer stuck their guns out the window and fired at the vehicles.

"Go around here and to hangar number sixteen," Mr. Yuan shouted, ducking as shots blasted at the car.

Major Winter followed the instructions as bullets hit the SUV. Major Winter was a good driver, and his swerving, evasive maneuvers made the North Koreans miss often. On top of it all, it began to rain. *Great*, Robert thought, but then realized this was positive. It might provide them with additional cover.

Major Winter raced along the hanger area, partially shielded by parked and taxiing planes from the North Korean army. Finally, he got to hangar number sixteen.

"These planes were meant to deliver our finished products from our country to the landing zones of the billionaires, as well as to some parts of China," Mr. Yuan explained, "but you don't know how to fly a plane."

"I do," Major Winter answered. "I was in the Navy Reserve for a few years doing cargo runs. It won't be an American plane, but if we're lucky it'll be close enough."

Major Winter parked the car in front of the door to the closed hangar, so that it could act as a barricade against intrusion. The group hurried out and Major Winter ran into the hangar.

Major Winter ran into the plane to begin setting it up.

Robert was the only one still in the car, and he looked over toward the North Korean soldiers. There were a few SUVs parked, with their doors open, around three hundred yards away, and the soldiers stood behind open doors and fired away. One of them had a microphone and was yelling something that Robert couldn't understand. Suddenly, many of them began to return to their cars.

"Go with Isabel to the plane!" Robert shouted, reloading his firearm.

Jennifer nodded and ducked, shielding Isabel from the gunfire around them. *It's not going to be enough time,* Robert thought, losing his faith slowly. *I have to do something . . .*

He looked quickly in the trunk of the car and saw a small bag. Since the car they stole was a military vehicle, he hoped the bag would have something useful inside it. *Yes!* Two old fragment grenades were inside.

Robert grabbed them and got into the car and turned on the ignition. He hoped it still worked despite the bullets now lodged inside it. Fortunately, the car roared to life. Robert aimed his SUV directly at the oncoming North Korean SUVs.

Robert yelled as loud as he could to release some stress and threw a grenade out of the window. He then started counting the seconds of the grenade. *Four, five, six* . . . he counted in his head, until the grenade exploded on the cement in front of him. Bullets were flying toward him again now. The cars would be on him soon; they were only few hundred yards away. Robert felt his blood pumping like battery acid through his body.

Then, Robert put his foot on the gas. The SUV jerked forward. He pulled the pin out of the second grenade, and started counting. *One, two,* he thought. Suddenly the windshield spider-webbed and he couldn't see a thing. Robert swore. He threw the grenade in the backseat, as close to the fuel tank as he could.

Four . . .

Once he reached *five* he opened the car door,

flung the transmission into neutral, and jumped out of the car, his old body hitting the ground with a painfully bone-crushing finality.

Robert, through his damp, blood-stained hair, saw the car roll toward the line of North Koreans and explode in a blaze.

Robert groaned loudly and rolled onto his back. He'd never been in so much pain in his life. His back, his ribs, his shoulder and his arm, his stomach, his legs—all of it felt broken.

He was losing his vision. He heard no more gunfire coming from the line of North Koreans, but in the distance he thought he could see more troops coming. His side hurt terribly, and he moved his arm down to his stomach, and felt a warm pool of blood where his stomach should have been. He tried to get up but it was no use; his leg was broken from jumping out of the car. Robert watched as the hangar door opened and an ancient cargo plane taxied out onto the runway.

"Dad! Robert! Robert Miller!" Jennifer cried from

the door of the plane, which moved slowly toward him. The hatch was open and the steps were still down.

Robert showed them his palm, which was red with blood, but they didn't listen to his signs of "leave." Robert looked back at the oncoming troops. Then Major Winter ran down toward him and picked him up. He remembered thinking, *fly the plane, Anton, fly the plane. If you're picking me up, who's flying the plane?* Then he lost consciousness . . .

Robert Miller's eyes were half-open, half-closed. They were in the air now. He could picture the plane flying over the Yellow Sea. His daughter held his hands. He could see little Isabel. *She looks so beautiful* . . . Robert thought blissfully.

10

CARDS

December 18, 2018, Los Alamos, New Mexico
Day Fifteen Post-Impact

"Can you believe that just three years ago," Jeremy asked Dustin, "we were all wondering where we were going to college and thinking about where to party on the weekend?"

They were standing outside the lobby of the National Laboratory, looking out over the horizon of their new alien landscape.

"I can't believe it's really over," Dustin said. "The comets have finally done their damage. After all that anticipation."

Jeremy looked over at his friend with raised eyebrows.

"My friend," he said, "it's only just beginning. Now is the time we have to rebuild our world."

They had heard that Secretary Brighton was calling for a census of the United States and spreading the word that order would return to the States. Once they had an accurate census, they would know better how much land they would need to cultivate and what food security pressures they would face.

"Are you going to take part in the census?" Dustin asked. "Are you going to go and try to find survivors?"

"Not for the next year or two at least," Jeremy explained. "I'm going to have a child to think about—little Norman. What about you?"

"Maybe I was thinking about it. But honestly I think it would be the last thing Karina would want to do."

"You would want her to go with you?"

"Well, yeah."

Jeremy learned from the government that the engineers on the billionaire's Ark had been unable to escape debris from the comet-Moon impact. They had been so focused on trying to somehow blast the smaller comet into orbit in order to mine its natural resources that they'd failed to try to change their own course. Suri told Jeremy that at least sixteen escape pods had been successfully ejected to Earth, though it would be impossible to know if those inside had survived the voyage. *The vicissitudes of fate*, Jeremy thought. *Their greed had made them billionaires, and it was that very same greed that killed them.* He knew it was unlikely, but he hoped that somehow Janice managed to be one of the lucky few to escape.

Secretary Brighton exited the lobby doors to smoke a cigarette outside. They all stood together, surveying the hazy horizon.

"Do you smoke?" the secretary asked Jeremy.

"No."

"Good. It'll give you cancer."

"Then why are you doing it?" Jeremy responded.

"Well, when I was younger, before it was so obvious it was a bad habit, I just did it because everyone did. Now, I am addicted, but I'll only permit myself one after great tragedies and great accomplishments. Recently, those events have been a bit ubiquitous, for better or worse."

The three stood outside and watched the noonday Sun pulverize the New Mexico hills, and the valley where they now stood.

Then, in the distance, Jeremy saw an aircraft flying in the horizon.

At first, Jeremy thought nothing of it—airplanes weren't anything special in the Old World—but then he realized that he hadn't seen a plane in the air for . . . well, a long time.

"Do you think that plane might be dangerous?" Jeremy wondered if the anarchists had commandeered planes and were now mounting a new offensive or something.

Secretary Brighton squinted in the sunlight through his sunglasses, peering at the swift birdlike shadow in the sky.

"No, in fact, it looks like an old AN-124," the

secretary said, before adding, "A Russian cargo plane."

"It looks like it's heading this way," Dustin said nervously.

Secretary Brighton flicked his cigarette onto the ground and rushed back inside, Jeremy at his coat-tails. He barked some orders at an army officer and in a minute there was a Humvee in front of the lobby. He hopped in.

"Wait," Jeremy called. "Can we come with you?"

Secretary Brighton thought for a moment. "There's room, but it's your neck if something's amiss."

Dustin didn't look so enthused.

"Go ahead," he said. "I think I'll wait back here."

Jeremy nodded and ran into the car, putting on his seatbelt in the back. There were two other armed guards inside it. Secretary Brighton told the driver to move to the other side because he wanted to drive. At first the guard hesitated, but then remember-ing his rank, changed positions without speaking.

Secretary Brighton threw the car into gear and the Humvee lurched forward. They sped off to the airstrip, the Humvee kicking up dust.

"Who do you think it is? A Russian diplomat, maybe?" Jeremy asked.

"They wouldn't take a cargo plane. I don't know," Secretary Brighton said, his jaw tense.

It took ten minutes for them to arrive at the airstrip, where some guards were awaiting instructions with their weapons drawn.

Jeremy hopped out, expecting to see one of two things: an emissary from Russia coming to the United States on a diplomatic mission, or even though he knew it wasn't likely, the return of Dr. Robert Miller. He hoped deeply for the latter.

As the plane taxied out toward the small group of hangars at the Los Alamos Municipal Airport, Jeremy tried to look in the small windows along the body of the plane. He could not see anyone initially, and when he did he only spied the tops of a few heads.

Then, the plane ceased to taxi and as the cabin depressurized a few soldiers stood near where the stairs would descend to the ground. Secretary Brighton and Jeremy Genser stood behind the soldiers, ready to welcome the visitors. Then, someone appeared from the plane.

A woman with long black hair holding a small girl by the hand walked down the steps. She had wide-set eyes and looked wan and wore tattered dark-grey prisoner's clothes. Jeremy focused on the woman, trying to figure out if he recognized her face or the little girl's, and although their visages did spark some recognition, he realized that he did not know them. *They look familiar, though,* Jeremy thought. *Where do I know her from?*

As they descended the steps, they looked quite sad and dejected. They held their heads low and they did not protect their faces from the punishing sunlight. The soldiers did not lower their weapons. Then, a familiar face appeared in the plane.

"That's Major Winter!" Jeremy told Secretary Brighton, explaining how he knew the man.

"Dr. Miller must be on the plane, then," Secretary Brighton said excitedly, betraying his normal stoic demeanor.

But as Major Winter walked down the steps, he turned around and helped a man yet unseen in the plane carry a stretcher down the steps. On the stretcher, covered in blood, lay the body of the most brilliant astrophysicist of his generation, and the savior of the human race.

Jeremy gasped and Secretary Brighton's muscles tightened. They rushed over to the plane, taking in the scene around them and trying to deduce what happened. The man carrying the stretcher with Dr. Miller was a small bespectacled Korean man, who looked to be mourning Dr. Miller as well. Secretary Brighton yelled at the soldiers to call for the medic, who was nearly upon the body already.

As the medic began to run diagnostics, Major Winter put a hand on his shoulder, and spoke. "He died on the way from North Korea, around ten hours ago."

The medic, however, still tried listening to a heartbeat. But when seeing Robert's stomach, he looked over at Secretary Brighton, shaking his head.

Brighton looked over at the woman with the small girl, standing in a prisoner's clothes, and then over to Major Winter, who was dressed much like Dr. Miller, both in the North Korean totalitarian-esque jumpsuits. Then he looked over at the North Korean, whose sad and anxious face betrayed nothing.

"What's your name, miss?" Secretary Brighton asked.

"Jennifer. I'm Jennifer Miller, and this is Isabel," Jennifer responded, hugging Isabel in the process.

That must be Dr. Miller's daughter, Jeremy reasoned.

Jeremy saw that the soldiers were eying the North Korean nervously.

"What happened, Major?" Brighton asked Major

Winter, beckoning for the Humvee to be driven closer. "Let's go back toward the base. You can explain what happened on the way."

Major Winter did not protest when Secretary Brighton ordered the North Korean to go in a different car. Jeremy silently followed Major Winter and Secretary Brighton back to the Humvee. *Dr. Miller is gone*, Jeremy thought. It was the only notion that entered his mind.

As they drove back to base, Major Winter told Secretary Brighton everything that happened in the last few weeks in North Korea, and Secretary Brighton took notes. Jeremy sat in a daze, feeling overcome with sadness at the death of Robert Miller. The fact that Major Winter described Dr. Miller's death as valiant and heroic did little to console him. He simply sat next to Major Winter on the drive back to the National Laboratory and looked straight ahead.

When they got back Jeremy excused himself to tell the news to Anna, whom he hoped was alone instead of having the company of Dustin and Karina. He got his wish.

"I have some sad news, Anna," Jeremy began, and then told Anna the story of Dr. Miller's heroic efforts to save his daughter.

Tears sprang into Anna's eyes. "I can't believe that they found his daughter and tried to blackmail him. So terrible, after all he did."

"Yeah," Jeremy said, before he began to cry quietly. It was uncontrolled and began in a whimper but ended torrentially, with Anna joining him in agony. Jeremy felt like it was a final straw—that after everything, he thought that a little bit of luck would bring Dr. Miller back.

"He did what he thought was right," Anna said, trying to wipe away her tears. "To save his family."

Jeremy nodded, more to convince himself than anyone else. They sat quietly together for a time, not saying anything.

"Jeremy, you know how we still need a name for our son?"

"Yeah?"

"What do you think about Robert?"

Jeremy smiled. He loved the idea.

. . .

Suri refused to believe that Robert was dead. She refused to believe that the man with whom she had worked to save the world for three years had sacrificed his life for his daughter. She stayed in her room and cried for a long time. She refused to see anyone or to work. Mostly, she slept. It was unthinkable that after all they had been through, her coworker, her idol was really gone. *He was like a father figure to me . . .* she lamented. On the third day of grieving, she came to a conclusion: *Robert wouldn't want me to just sit around,* she thought. *He'd tell me to get out there and make sure to rebuild the Earth.*

She figured it was necessary that she go speak with Dr. Miller's daughter as well and offer her condolences. She made her way down the residence wing and found their room, then knocked on the door.

"Come in," a voice called.

Suri found both Isabel and Jennifer sitting upright playing a card game on a hospital bed.

"What's this?" Suri asked, watching. The game seemed to require quick hand speed.

"Double solitaire. It's a wonderful game," Jennifer said, looking up briefly as Isabel took advantage of her mother's neglect.

Jennifer paused the game and asked if Isabel could explain the game to Suri, which she did.

"It's just like normal solitaire, where you try to get all the cards in the seven rows to move up to the four piles of suits, Aces first, above your seven rows: spades, clubs, diamonds, and hearts. Mommy and I each have a separate deck. You can only put a two on an Ace, and a four on a three, but they must be the same suit.

"The only difference is that the 'Aces' piles are

playable for both of us. Sometimes we both have the card—like a three of clubs—and whoever puts their three of clubs on the 'clubs' stack wins!"

To show this, Isabel slammed a three of clubs on her mother's clubs stack, flashing a taunting smile at her mother.

"Exactly," Jennifer said, smiling, and they continued playing.

Suri still didn't really understand the game but watched as the mother and daughter played together.

When the game ended, Suri tried to tell Jennifer how much her father meant to her, the country, and the world, but it came out a little jumbled.

"Don't forget he saved my life," Jennifer said.

"Right. Well, I guess I just wanted to tell you that without his work we probably wouldn't be here, any of us, in the entire world. He meant a lot to me."

Jennifer nodded, and then turned to her daughter.

"Honey," Jennifer said, putting a hand on Isabel's

shoulder, "Suri and I are going to step outside. Are you okay to set up the next game by yourself?"

"Sure!" Isabel said, beginning to separate the two card decks again.

Suri and Jennifer walked outside and without warning, Suri began to cry again and hugged Jennifer.

"I'm sorry, I know that you guys had a hard relationship," Suri sobbed. "But you should know that he did really love you. He told me that many times while we worked together."

At this, Jennifer started to cry, too. They hugged until Isabel called inside for her mother to come back and play another game.

"He told me once about you," Jennifer said. "He said that it was really nice to work with you, and told me you're really gifted. He said that no one would have been able to do the work they did without your help."

"Wow, thanks," Suri answered.

"Do you want to come in and sit with us?" Jennifer offered.

"Sure, sounds nice."

Suri walked in and grabbed a chair, watching the mother and daughter play double solitaire until the Sun dropped behind the Los Alamos hills in the distance.

11

NEW BEGINNINGS

February 27, Year 0 Post-Comet (PC),
Los Alamos National Laboratory

Suri busied herself with the construction of new satellites and rockets, which would need to be launched into space again. She shifted her focus to this at the request of Secretary Brighton, who put her in charge of rebuilding the United States' communications programs.

"Suri?" a voice called from behind her office.

"Come in," she called cheerfully, finishing the line of code she was working on before looking up.

Secretary Brighton slid into the seat in front of her. "President Chaplin and I are going to award you and Robert the Presidential Medal of Freedom and the Congressional Medal of Honor for your work," Secretary Brighton said. "I want to make sure that the people of the United States—and the world for that matter—know who saved life on Earth. I want them to know that it wasn't some divine intervention that saved us, or something ridiculous. I want the American people to know the names Robert Miller and Suri Lahdka for all time. Hell, if I could put your faces on the bills we use, and the clothes we wear I would.

"An awards ceremony is being planned for two months' time. I wanted to let you know personally my appreciation for your and Robert's work and dedication. The human race is alive because of you."

"Thank you, sir. That means a lot," Suri said, blushing considerably. "I was just trying to do my best."

"Well, your best saved the world. Not many people can say that. Dr. Rhodes will be getting the full honors as well. We might even find a place for her on Mount Rushmore."

Secretary Brighton then shook Suri's hand warmly, and she could have sworn she saw a tear escaping the politician's eye. Dr. Rhodes had sacrificed herself for the human race. She'd turned the Vishnu spacecraft into a bomb and steered the comet into the Moon successfully.

"Are you okay, sir?" Suri asked.

Secretary Brighton smiled. "I'm fine, Suri. It's just been a long few years, hasn't it?"

"Yes, sir, it really has."

Suri got back to working on the code, but felt distracted by Secretary Brighton's words. Her mind suddenly shifted to the many people who had died, and the few from the Ark that still survived. The government knew the truth about the conspiracy to hurt the chances of stopping the comet, and many had felt it was karmic—a perfect "what comes around, goes around" situation. Suri learned that some of the billionaires had lived—exactly twenty of them in fact. Considering there were around four hundred who left Earth, this was a small number indeed. Thus far all of them were in hiding, which was probably best. A part of her felt that it served them right after abandoning their fellow people and planet instead of fighting to save it.

. . .

Due to the starvation, anarchy, and the direct result of the impact's megatsunami and heat explosion, the United States was now comprised of around one hundred and thirty million people, a loss of around sixty percent of its population. Many of the survivors were spread out across the entire United States, living in self-made bunkers, feeding themselves on anything they could find. Though it had succumbed to anarchy, the U.S.'s state of hyper-paranoia and fear surrounding nuclear fallout during the Cold War with Russia led citizens to build tons of bomb shelters. These bomb shelters saved millions of lives. Likewise, Russia also managed to save a good chunk of its population.

The rest of the world was not so lucky. Europe's population west of Russia had been reduced to almost zero due to its proximity to the initial impact. The Air Force had flown reconnaissance missions over the previously inhabited countries in the past four months and had discovered frighteningly that few people had survived. Tragically, East Asia and India suffered the worst from the natural disaster—around eighty percent of their population had perished. In the entire world, it was estimated that only around half of the population had survived. Around three and a half billion people had perished, and horrifyingly, starvation would only increase the despair.

President Chaplin was still Chief Executive of the United States, and she implemented the Development Act. With the newly formed Council to Rebuild Infrastructure, or CRI, every able-bodied person found in the United States was put to work to rebuild the country. Chaplin and Brighton created teams of scientists and engineers to make proposals detailing exactly how they should proceed. Gerald Jan would have been particularly prescient in this capacity had he still been alive, but the CRI worked very much in his image.

Many of his coworkers and employees continued to advise on the plans for rebuilding infrastructure. Solar panel grids were being built throughout the United States.

In order to avoid making the same mistakes as in the past, the electric infrastructure was set up to function primarily with solar energy. There were charging station for cars being set up all over the country. The U.S. even passed a law that prohibited the commercial sale of products that burned fuel inefficiently.

There was a branch within NASA that would focus on colonizing Mars, in the incredibly unlikely event that a future comet threatened the Earth. North Korea was the only true enemy of the United States, and even China refused to back them after the kidnapping of Dr. Miller was publicized. Unlike the

United States, North Korea was now completely on its own.

Of course, a massive amount of clean-up had to be undertaken before any rebuilding could take place. The entire eastern seaboard had been destroyed by the tsunami, and the rising temperatures had melted the polar ice caps, so sea levels had risen an incredible ninety feet. Over two-thirds of Florida was underwater, and most of the country's coastline was uninhabitable.

The Development Act had rebuilt radio towers to incorporate the entire United States. Speaking from Los Alamos, President Chaplin gave her first presidential address in two years on AM 1050. She gave an address to the American people, and then spoke to the United States every day for two weeks.

As she spoke through the antiquated technology, President Chaplin urged the American public to reaffirm their belief in their country, in democracy, and in the continued preservation of the human race. Pragmatically, she informed them of the plan to grow crops using seeds from the Svalbard Global Seed Vault and that food deliveries to several locations around the United States would begin, helping anyone struggling to feed their families or themselves.

Other countries were doing similar things. Canadian survivors were slowly rebuilding their country as well. In Africa, however, things were much worse. The war-torn continent had become a wasteland. Many of the refugees from Europe had landed in North Africa, and due to starvation after the first comet hit, many had not survived.

Yet, glimmers of hope existed. From the Air Force flybys in the Great Lakes region of Sub-Saharan Africa, pilots saw lights from fires below. The Great Lakes region—home to some of the richest mineral deposits in the world—was a network of underground mines, and people had used those mines to shield themselves from the secondary effects of the comet, until it was safe to live above ground again.

In the Arabian Peninsula, sadly, only the citizens who could afford to go underground survived.

The scientists working for the government had proven that the modified crops were safe to eat. This was extremely good news, as they were also the only crops that could grow until the ozone layer regenerated, assuming it could.

Several scientific predictions turned out to be false. One was the idea that the Earth would cool after an impact, from the shade of debris jettisoned into the atmosphere, but that turned out to be wrong. There was also the false prediction that the initial heat generated from the comet impact would last for six months, but this also turned out to be untrue.

Dustin had taken it upon himself to join in the effort to stabilize the country. President Chaplin had asked for volunteers to become some sort of Domestic Ambassadors, traveling throughout the United States to deliver food, seeds, and information to people struggling to feed themselves in the new age. Dustin enthusiastically accepted. *It'll be my second job in the industry,* he thought jokingly, remembering his work as a Seed Ambassador for the Global Seed Vault. He had just returned from a trip to southern California with his boss, Major Winter, who had also volunteered. On their next mission, Dustin and Major Winter were to travel to Houston to set up a food distribution center.

Major Winter had actually been offered a promotion. General Diaz offered him the new Secretary of DFNID, the Department of Food and Necessary Item Distribution.

"Thank you for the opportunity, General, but I must respectfully decline. My place is out on the front lines," he had said warmly, thanking General Diaz for the offer.

Major Winter was thus in charge of the implementation and distribution strategy for the DNFID.

One day in the end of February in Year 0 PC, Jeremy, Anna, Karina, and Dustin were all sitting in the cafeteria in Los Alamos, eating the new genetically modified vegetable soup for dinner.

"I never thought vegetable soup could taste so good," Dustin exclaimed, smacking his lips.

"Comes after not eating real food for about a year!" Karina laughed.

"It's really amazing what the government is doing now," Anna mused. "The solar panel project and the windmills in the Midwest; it seems like it's definitely a lot easier to change the country to clean energy now, right?"

The group agreed, and Jeremy said, "I guess, but it's a sad upside to everything that's happened. When I spoke with Suri, she said they were trying to make these new kinds of satellites that can provide internet access to people on the ground. With the old infrastructure basically destroyed, they can start from scratch."

Spirits were high. Despite everything, they had all survived what some believed an apocalypse. In fact, they did better than survive; they were happy.

12

ROBERT

March 29, Year 0 PC,
Los Alamos National Laboratory

Jeremy awoke to Anna slapping him roughly across the face.

"Ow! Anna, what the—"

What felt like a punch in the face was actually a slap. Anna's water had broken and she was going into labor.

"Oh, Anna, is it time?!" he said, halfway in between excitement and anxiety.

"Yes, you idiot, I—" Anna began, before doubling over in pain. "Jeremy! Go get someone!"

"Right," Jeremy answered, scrambling to get

his head in the right place. *It's finally happening!* he thought in nervous apprehension.

Jeremy then stood up and stumbled due to a mild head-rush from standing up so quickly. Then, he ran to Dr. Patricks's room. He pounded on the door, impatient for the doctor to wake up.

After what seemed like minutes the woman opened the door.

"Yes?"

"I think Anna's going into labor!" Jeremy said quickly.

The doctor rubbed the sleep from her eyes as she slowly woke up.

"Alright," the doctor said, yawning. "Can she walk?"

"Yes, I think so."

"Take her to the hospital wing and I'll meet you both there soon." She must have seen the panicked look on his face because she added, "She's going to be fine."

Jeremy nodded, his heart racing, and ran back

towards his room to help Anna, but she was already walking toward the hospital wing.

"I don't want to do this," she moaned, wincing and clutching her stomach.

Jeremy didn't exactly know how to console her. What could he say?

"Well, a lot of people have gone through it before. I'm sure it's not that bad."

Anna looked like she was about to slap him across the face again, but another contraction forced her concentration to move elsewhere.

"I'll be by your side the entire time," Jeremy said. "You can dig your nails into my arm when something hurts. That way, we'll go through it together, okay?"

Jeremy's response did make Anna feel better, and she managed a grim smile, and together they walked to the hospital.

The next hours were tough on Anna, and Jeremy often felt as though he didn't know what he should do. As the hours went by, his arm had more and more claw wounds in it from Anna's nails. At two hours, Dr. Patricks left the birthing room. Apparently another doctor needed help setting a leg.

"When will you be back?" Jeremy asked.

"Fifteen minutes at the most. Don't worry, she's doing fine," she replied, and rushed out of the room.

Ten minutes later Anna grunted in pain again. "I can't do this, Jer!" she gasped. "Can't I have . . . something for the—" another contraction stole her breath and she looked like she might pass out. "Jeremy, go get Dr. Patricks," she wailed. "Please."

Desperate to help Anna, Jeremy nodded and found Dr. Patricks outside the room. "I think Anna's going to die!" he said. "She's begging for something for the pain. Can't you give her an epidural?" he pleaded.

"Jeremy," Dr. Patricks replied, "back before the comet I worked as a family doctor. I know how it's done but I wouldn't be comfortable performing such a procedure. It's way too risky. I can give her some

Demerol now, but it's not good to give her anything directly before the birth, for the safety of the baby."

"Demerol will help, then?" Jeremy asked, relieved.

"Somewhat. It'll take the edge off."

Jeremy's hope deflated. "So, she's still going to be in pain?"

Dr. Patricks looked sideways at Jeremy. "She's giving birth, Jeremy. Of course she's going to be in pain."

Jeremy grimaced, frustrated that there was so little he could do. He didn't want to see Anna hurting like this.

Jeremy rubbed his arm with Anna's red marks on it and went back into her room. He hadn't known Anna could grip that hard, but certainly the red marks in his arm made him reconsider allowing her to do it. Dr. Patricks walked in and explained the situation to Anna.

"It's fine," Anna responded. She seemed to have found some kind of inner strength while Jeremy was talking with Dr. Patricks. "Don't drug me up. I want to remember."

Jeremy looked impressed at his girlfriend. *She can handle more pain than me,* he thought. He remembered the most painful sports injury he had ever received—tearing his anterior cruciate ligament, or ACL, in a basketball game in high school. There had been a split-second blinding flash of pain as his knee bent backwards unnaturally before he collapsed to the ground. After the incident, and the painful knee tests afterwards, Jeremy wanted to be entirely alone to recuperate and deal with the pain in his own way. It would endlessly annoy him when he would be consoled with a touch on the shoulder or a pitying gaze.

Then Dr. Patricks told Anna that it was time to push. In a flash, the bed was readied, nurses swarmed into the room, the lights were brightened. Jeremy gripped Anna's hand, watching her endure what he imagined was a constant, full-bodied, and unceasing pain, and thought that all his experiences with pain were meaningless compared to hers. The doctor told her to push and Jeremy could not imagine the pain that it was causing her, though she'd started to make his arm bleed from her nails. Jeremy told Anna to push; he felt like if he yelled it would make the baby come faster.

"You're doing great, Anna," Dr. Patricks said as Anna lay back, panting.

Seeing Anna's tired, red face made Jeremy wish they could share the pain together. The doctor told Anna to push one more time, and Anna strained, her whole body curling forward. When Jeremy saw the baby come out of Anna he was speechless, his eyes wide, seeing a true human miracle.

It was a boy!

Just like that, Anna and Jeremy were parents. Anna held a new baby boy in her arms.

"Congratulations," Dr. Patricks said warmly.

Anna looked up at Jeremy and said, "What do you think?"

"Wow."

It was all Jeremy could say. It was all so unbelievable, and he felt such an incredible shifting of emotions: elation, fear, hope, anxiety, joy, pride. Most of all, he felt love, in that moment, towering over all other emotions. This little thing was a part of him, and a part of Anna. And now, it was a part of this new world.

"He's . . . " he answered, "beautiful."

"You want to hold him?" a tired Anna whispered.

Anna held out the baby for Jeremy to take and he held his son. From the moment he held his son his emotion magnified exponentially. Looking down at his son he felt intense euphoria, a closeness with the majestic and divine that he'd never felt before. He was holding his *own son*. There was no comparable feeling to it in the entire world.

"He's lighter than I'd thought he'd be," Jeremy said.

"That's because you didn't just push him out of yourself," Anna joked.

Jeremy smiled.

Suddenly, Anna started to cry.

"What's wrong?" Jeremy asked, worried, looking toward Dr. Patricks.

"Nothing, nothing," Anna sobbed. "I'm just so happy. Little Robert Genser just took his first step of independence."

That made Jeremy tear up, too, and he handed Robert back to Anna.

"Welcome to the new world, little guy," Jeremy smiled.

. . .

One month later, Jeremy sat in his room, tired and sore from a hard day's work.

He sat at the little makeshift desk, relaxing. He kissed little Robby in his crib, who was making weird grunting noises while kicking his legs.

"How's it going, Robby?" he asked.

Robby smiled, and Jeremy sat down at his desk again, taking out a piece of paper. Even though he didn't think of himself as the best writer, he figured that someone had to write the story of the man who saved the world. He stared at the blank page, tapping it with the lead of his pencil. Finally, to the sounds of Robby making baby noises, he began to write:

Dr. Robert Miller: Savior of the Human Race

Chapter One